BOJANGLE'S DANCE

By M.C. Keesee

Copyright

ISBN: 978-1-0682754-0-1

Published by
The Book Publisher
www.thebookpublisher.co

CHAPTER 1

The First Step

The two figures moved like ghosts through the abandoned streets, their footsteps echoing against weathered storefronts with boarded windows and faded signs. The older one, who resembled a down-on-his-luck Santa with snow-white hair and weathered hands tucked into worn pockets, walked beside his younger companion, a towering presence whose dark skin gleamed with a thin sheen of perspiration despite the chill in the morning air. His broad shoulders seemed to cast shadows of their own as they walked in practiced silence. The town seemed to have exhaled its last breath years ago, leaving behind only the hollow skeleton of what it once was. Few establishments showed signs of life between the crumbling facades and weed-cracked sidewalks. They were the only heartbeats in this forgotten place.

"I don't mean to second-guess you, Mr. Bojangle, but are you sure about this?" Marcus "Big Mac" Mackensie curved his hand against his forehead, more to block out what passed as scenery than against the early morning sunlight that crept up through the city's shadows. A scar ran like a broken road down his forehead, across his eye, and down into his cheek. This place reminded him of a neighborhood in a distant memory. The blade that left that scar and nearly left him blind was only one of them. "Maybe we should…"

"Start somewhere smaller." The old man beside him finished the sentence for him. "With problems that look less intimidating? Somewhere that pretends to be a little less hostile?" Mr. Bojangle smiled with delight. "No, Mac. We're right where we need to be. We've done all the research. We know the plans. Starting over somewhere else would be the wrong call. Besides, Sarah brought one of her smiles to my dreams last night. She and I danced under a streetlight just like that one over there, with the kids laughing just out of sight. This is the right place. Just look for it, Mac." There was an air of awe in Bo's words when he spoke again. "Really look at it."

Mac knew what was really meant. He had to see the dream, not the current state of things. That was something that hadn't come easily at first. Sometimes, like now, it still didn't. He always felt the need to protect Mr. Bojangle and everything the older man stood for. Standing on the broken sidewalk beneath a shattered streetlight, staring at three stories of graffiti-covered brick squatting beside a vacant lot that looked more like a scab over some puss-filled wound, reminded him too much of the dangers he had grown up with. Instinct screamed that he needed to talk his friend out of calling this place home. This place was too far gone, too lost in the darkness.

Then, Bo turned that smile his way. It was the same smile he had first seen the day his old life had ended, and this new one had begun. Mac smiled back. He couldn't help it. That was what Robert "Bo" Jangle did to people. His smile lifted the weight of the world from them and made hope rush in to fill the void it left behind.

"It's built like an ox," Big Mac, or Mac to most, said as the dream of what this place would be, what Mr. Bojangle would coax it into becoming, took shape under the watery light of the new day.

"Kind of like you, my friend," Bo laughed with delight. "And its heart is just as strong. I can feel it. Can't believe we picked it up in the bankruptcy auction for so cheap. Back in its day, it was the old Meridian factory. Most of these buildings around here were part of it. It'll remember how to be something great again soon enough. A different kind of great this time. Close your eyes and see it, Mac."

And just like that, Marcus Mackensie saw the dream as clear

as day. All of the ideas, the buildings, all of the notes and lists, and every last detail of Mr. Bojangle's monumental undertaking crushed the reality standing before him and replaced it with what would be.

"CJ called earlier," Mac said as he considered a couple of small changes that would have big effects down the road. Flowers, he thought. Big planters full of them out front to soften the boxy lines of the building. Maybe some window boxes, too. He let the corner of his mouth twitch up in amusement. Who would ever take him as someone who thought of flowers? "The inspector finally got around to admitting the inside is safe enough. So, we're cleared to start work. The electricity and water should be back in service sometime this afternoon."

"Then, it looks like we need to get our crew together, don't we?" Mr. Bojangle ran a hand down the snowy slope of his beard and stared at the old shed leaning against the back corner of the building. "He hasn't moved on, has he?"

"He's still there," Mac grinned. "He's going to hate giving up that shed, though. It might not look like much from the outside, but he's put a lot into his living space."

"Just think what he'll do when we unleash him on the rest." Bo's eyes twinkled with that mischievous twinkle. "Come on. Let's go poke around inside. With any luck, we can move in tonight and get this ball rolling."

They would be sleeping rough for a while, but that was nothing new. Bo didn't waste effort on his own comfort. Mac didn't either. Worn down wasn't the same as worn out in either of their minds. As long as there was a place to get out of the weather and a hot shower to wash away the grime at the end of the day, they were living large. Everything they needed was either tucked into a duffle bag or could be had quickly enough to suit their needs. Some people might not understand. That was okay. Big Mac and Mr. Bojangle did. The dream was bigger than either of them. All that mattered was bringing it to life.

CHAPTER 2

A New Song in the Air

The neighborhood was painted in hues of orange and red by the setting sun when the odd pair walked into Rosa's Restaurant. It had been a long day, and it was time to get a bite and relax. As Bojangle entered, his baggy pants and scraggly shirt were a sharp contrast to his warm, twinkling blue eyes and snow-white beard as he entered. Mac, following behind him, almost ducking through the doorway, flashed a big, overexaggerated smile. As a towering black man with muscles that seemed carved from stone and with that scar, he knew he had to try extra hard to change the atmosphere when he entered a room. He could make people nervous without even trying.

Trouble, Rosa thought at first glance, and nearly called Maria and Luis back into the kitchen to put some distance between her children and the newcomers. Something stopped her. She looked again, harder this time. There it was. There was something different about these two. Beneath the scar and the muscle, behind the white hair and the shabby clothes, was something far different from what she first saw. She felt a change in the air, and it was for good. Something good, wholesome, even. Rosa had seen so little of that lately that her breath caught on a longing sigh even before her brain registered the truth. They stood at her door, in sharp contrast to the empty husk of the place she called home.

"Maria," Rosa called and then motioned to the best booth she had to offer with her chin. "I'll put on some fresh coffee if our guests don't mind waiting for it."

Maria, ten years old and so proud of herself for being able to help her mother by finally being allowed to carry plates and pour coffee that she could barely keep from skipping through the restaurant while she did so, met the two men at the door. She was no slouch when it came to judging people for the soul she saw inside them, either. Whether it was a gift she was born with or something learned from living in a city where knowing the difference between good and bad was necessary for survival, she had honed it into a knowing that was far beyond her years.

Before she picked up the menus, she cocked her head and gave each of the men a blatant once-over. What she saw made her smile wide enough to show the gap where she had lost another baby tooth a few days ago.

"You're very tall," she said, grinning up at Mac. She turned, "And you look like Santa. Are you? Mom says I'm not supposed to be rude, but I think it's important to find some cookies and milk if you are."

"I'm Mr. Bojangle," came Bo's reply, flashing the most genuine smile. "And this is Marcus, but most folks call him Mac, or Big Mac." He paused and held his hand up as if to whisper, but let his voice carry. "You might think it's because he's so strong, but it's not; it's because his heart is so big…and he is a giant teddy bear. He'll even admit it to the right people."

Marcus nodded his face impassively, save for a softening around his eyes.

"Looks like you came to the right spot," Maria laughed as she grabbed two menus from the caddy beside the door. "I still think you might be Santa Claus. I just didn't know elves were so big. All of the Christmas books have pictures of them, even smaller than Luis, with pointed ears." She turned toward the kitchen and called out, "Mom, we need some cookies for later. Do we have any?"

"I'll see what I can do," Rosa answered with a chuckle.

"Maybe pie, instead?"

"Pie would be perfect," the bearded man sang out with a booming laugh that had Rosa second-guessing the impossibility of her daughter's declaration.

Rosa looked over to see how her eight-year-old son was reacting to all of this while she loaded the coffee pot. Her smile grew. Luis was staring from his makeshift fort in the corner booth with wide eyes and lips shaped into an awestruck O. She would let him keep that feeling as long as it would stick. It had been a long day, part of a string of long days that stretched back years. They could all use a little magic for as long as it wanted to hang around. If her children wanted to think that Santa and his giant elf had come to eat at her restaurant, what harm could it do? Besides, she had everyone in her sights and was ready to spring into action if the need arose. She, too, had learned things over the years. The most important one was that trust only went so far. When it came to her children, she kept a close watch. No one got near without her noticing..

The locals called the restaurant a "hole in the wall," but to Rosa Martinez, it was life itself. Not only hers, but the promise that her children would be taken care of and, eventually, their children, too. Her father had built his dream with the future in mind, before the city began to crumble around them after the factory closed. After he was gone, nostalgia and practicality kept it alive, even if some days Rosa felt like it might be better to pack up and go somewhere else. Where? She didn't know. All she knew was that the city she had loved her entire life was in trouble now. Big trouble. It wasn't the same place it had been when she was a child, playing outside the doors instead of in a corner booth. Her kids deserved better than what she feared they would find here if they stayed.

Another big, booming laugh erupted from her new guests, driving away the haunting chill of dread that had started settling into Rosa's bones over the past few years. For a moment, the little restaurant felt exactly the same as when she was small and her father let her make the tamales for the first time. She wasn't sure whether to laugh or cry. When neither happened, she let her eyes travel over the seating area again. Seeing that all was well, she went back to the tasks at hand.

"Order in," Maria announced after a twirling journey across the old linoleum to the counter. "And it's a big one!"

"Go get your math done while I get it ready, love." Rosa tried for a stern look but couldn't quite manage it. She knew it wasn't necessary, anyway. Maria was pulling in straight A's at school, even with long evening hours spent waiting tables, ringing up customers, and washing dishes.

Luis, too. His hands were too small to do much good, but the boy helped out as much as he could whenever he saw a problem. At the ripe old age of eight and a half, Luis was absolutely sure he wanted to be an engineer when he grew up. If his current attempts at fixing everything were any sign, Rosa didn't doubt he would achieve his goals. Her son saw the world differently. Even enveloped in the strange magic carried in with her current customers, Rosa could all but hear the wheels turning in Luis's brain. His broken toy car was the center of attention today. The tools laid out on the table beside it were just waiting for him to solve the puzzle of the repair at hand.

Rosa wondered what her mother would think about all of this when she came by to help close down for the night. Since the restaurant was a family affair, and the two gentlemen looked like they had settled in for the long run, Rosa was sure she would find out. Sofia Alverez had eyes like a hawk, a nose that could smell trouble ten miles away, and a no-nonsense disposition that made Rosa's overprotective nature look like she was carefree. It would be interesting. That much was inevitable.

Her restaurant was usually a quiet place where customers would sit, keep to themselves, eat food, and shuffle back into the night. Tonight, the atmosphere was different. Rosa watched the strange duo from the kitchen window as she prepared their meals. The older man engaged anyone who walked by, dropping compliments and laughing boisterously with his compadre. It was as if he were the king, holding court, or perhaps the jester. Rosa knew these guys were not from this area, but she was happy they had brought a little life to her sleepy restaurant.

A small smile played at the corners of her lips as she saw their reaction to the steaming plates Maria carefully set before them. She wished her mom would come in early so she could get caught up in the joy radiating through the restaurant tonight. It had been far too long since Rosa had heard her mother's laugh. She was sure that the music of it would sing out tonight once she arrived.

Distracted by the thought of her mother's long-past-due happiness, Rosa caught a movement from Luis's corner. He was trying not to get upset over his broken car. Rosa was about to intervene when the two men asked him what was wrong. He just held his car up as if that was enough information. The plastic wheel had snapped off, and with it, his dreams of racing it tomorrow. He was a shy kid who didn't say a lot, even when his mind was working overtime. Usually, that was Rosa's cue to give him a distraction.

The old man beckoned Luis over before Rosa could wash her hands. She hesitated. Maybe, just this once, it was okay to see what happened next. So far, the two men had been nothing but kind. They had given her no reason to worry. Still, she would watch just to be sure.

"May I?" Big Mac's deep voice was surprisingly gentle as he held out his massive hand. Luis hesitated, then scooted out of his booth and walked over to theirs. He placed the broken car in the big man's palm.

Mr. Bojangle winked at the boy. "You don't need to be afraid, my little friend. Mac here can fix anything. Just watch."

With hands that seemed too large for such delicate work, Mac carefully examined the toy. From his pocket, he produced a small tool kit - the kind that spoke of preparation, of expecting to find things that needed fixing.

Rosa watched from the kitchen window, thinking that one day, that would be Luis. He wouldn't be as big, of course, but a tool kit would be in his pocket, and the need to fix the broken things he found in the world would drive him. She relaxed again as her little one's face transformed from one of despair to one of joy. The sight of Luis leaning in to watch the repair, asking quiet questions the whole time Big Mac's hands worked, made her smile. When he tested the wheels before clutching the toy to his chest with a smile bright enough to light up even the darkest corner of the world, Rosa felt something old, ugly, and hard as stone crack inside her heart. Whatever was happening here was big. Bigger than just one plastic toy that would be able to race tomorrow. Bigger than her daughter's insistence that a bearded stranger and his hulking friend were something magical. Rosa wasn't sure what it was, but she knew that tomorrow looked a lot brighter because of it.

CHAPTER 3

Dancing in the Shadows

Spider leaned back against a dented mailbox across from the only restaurant with decent food left in his territory. The money in his pocket felt good. A full belly would feel better. Rosa's place always gave him that, and it didn't feel like it was ripping his guts apart two hours later. He had been looking forward to it all day long as he traded the little bags in his cargo pants for the roll of cash he'd have to hand over to Rico by midnight. He always hated that part of the day. His fingers got used to gripping the roll as it collected. The weight of the money felt natural as it rested against his thigh. Then, in a matter of seconds, it was gone, and he was left with a few crumpled bills instead. It pissed him off.

He felt his face twist as he watched the scene inside Rosa's from just beyond the cone of light cast by a streetlamp. Something was off. Way off. Things in there looked a bit too cheery for his liking.

"New faces," Spider muttered, running his tongue over his teeth. "Don't like new faces."

The two men with their asses parked in his booth didn't look like they were going to be new customers to add to his roll of cash, either. Whatever they were buying wasn't found in one of the little bags Rico handed him to sell every day. Spider could tell. Oh, there was hunger there. He could almost feel it nipping through the glass at him. He just didn't understand it. If pushed, Spider wouldn't even be able to explain how he knew it was there. It was just a feeling in his rumbling gut. Desire. Need. Desperation in its own way, just not in the way Spider was used to seeing. All of those things sat with the old man and his large friend inside Rosa's food joint.

It would be easy enough to wipe the stupid smile off the old man's mouth and leave it trickling down his beard. Spider could teach him the lessons he needed to learn if he thought he was going to stick around.

The big guy was a different story. The hair prickled on the back of Spider's neck as those dark eyes, one slashed across with a scar that made the one Rico sported look tiny, turned to scan the growing darkness beyond the window that separated them. Spider knew a thug when he saw one. Hell, he had been on the receiving end of fists more than once since he joined Rico's crew. That was the problem with wanting more than he was given. He'd learned his lesson, though. The next time he went up against a monster like that, he would be ready.

Tonight wasn't the night, growling stomach or not. Rosa could keep her damned tamales. He had other options that would let him unload the rest of his stash in the process. He could even get a little extra for reminding the oncoming shift at the gas station how one little accident could bring it all down around their ears. He made sure that didn't happen, didn't he? His corner, his street, his responsibility, and one little gas station that could just as easily turn into a crater if everybody didn't do their part.

He turned on his heel and tucked his hands into his pockets, fingers automatically wrapping around that roll of cash he would keep for himself one of these days.

"Not tonight," he muttered over his shoulder as the darkness swallowed him.

He'd have to tell Rico about the newcomers. He should make the call now instead of waiting. The thing was, he wanted to know more first. There was still a chance the old man and his muscle were just passing through. No sense in crying wolf if that was the case. No sense in rocking the boat, either. Not when Spider had spent the last few weeks giving some serious thought to his place in the organization and how he might be able to get himself a good promotion.

"Rico's going soft," he reminded himself, although not loud enough for anyone tucked out of sight to hear. He wasn't stupid enough for that by a long shot. Soft or not, Rico kept a close eye on his crew and had them keep even more eyes on each other. That was the nature of the business. "Rosa's place is proof of that."

She was getting off scot-free in the protection department. That was another thing that nobody in the crew said out loud anymore. Not since Rico "Scar" Morales sent his former lieutenant to the hospital a year ago. Chigs came out of it carrying a limp and a demotion to what they all called the mail room, handling product intake instead of the boss's security.

It wasn't Rosa who inspired the lead pipe that busted Chigs' kneecap. She was pretty enough, but too old to be of any real use beyond doling out food. It was her damned kids. For some reason, the boss didn't want them touched. Not now. Not later. Not ever. Kids were the great and mighty Scar's Achilles' heel. Hell, he'd gotten to the point where he wouldn't even add to the ranks if a candidate was under seventeen. Those in the know whispered that their ruthless leader was pulled into the life before his voice cracked its way into puberty, and he just didn't have the stomach to do the same to some other street kid.

The thing was, that's all any of those precious little babies he thought so highly of had in the way of options around here. That or wasting away, waiting to be old enough to convince one of the local businesses that were left to pay them pennies for their time. If Spider were running things, he'd pull them in early and fill their pockets enough to keep them jumping when he said jump. That's how it was supposed to be. The little assholes stayed in line better when they were too small to kick up a fight when they didn't get their way. They didn't serve the same kind of time when they got busted, either. It was a win all the way around in Spider's book.

He shuffled into the convenience store and watched as the cashiers instantly averted their eyes. That gave him some satisfaction. More than he had felt since rounding the corner and seeing Rosa's brats jumping around like they didn't have a care in the world.

He filled a basket with whatever looked good and listened for the gangly clerk to do the right thing. When he heard the door swing open and the scrape of stool legs on the concrete floor, Spider's satisfaction grew; he had taught them well. Grabbing the stool without so much as a glance at the two sheep behind the counter, he carried his haul out front and got down to filling the rumbling hole in his gut while he waited for his next customer. He was short on supply, but there was enough left to make it worth his while, and anyone buying this late would be willing to take what they could get for whatever he wanted to charge them. Rico didn't need to know about the extra, either. Spider knew how to keep his rainy day fund off the radar.

"Hey, Spider." Now, here was the kind of desperation that Spider understood. The girl reeked of it under her cheap perfume. The fingernails raking over her arm were ragged, the polish chipped. She was one of his regulars when she could find the cash. From the look in her eyes as she turned them up, from a careful study of her cheap vinyl boots, tonight wasn't her night.

"Don't even try it, Avril. I ain't your bank, and you still haven't paid for that bump you begged me for last week. And I don't feel like taking trade tonight. You look too rough." He smirked. It was good to remind someone just how much he could make them squirm. "Go find someone to foot the bill or deal with the demons. I don't care which. Just don't come to me when you got the itch but not the scratch. How much you think you can make out there with a busted jaw? That's what you're gonna get if you come beggin' again."

Her face crumpled, her lower lip quivering as she hobbled away on her crappy boots without any more argument. This was the city that Spider understood. It was simple. Feeding the need meant finding the cash. No meant no. It didn't matter whether it was the cashiers inside who knew that anything in the store was his for the taking or the stupid junky slut who knew better than to ask twice - should have known better to ask the first time, but Spider could let that slide. It was the law of supply and demand.

He thought of Rosa's place again and scowled. Whatever was going on there right now didn't fit. Not here. Those two guys didn't fit well into this neighborhood. He didn't want to wait. He pulled out his phone and stared at it before dialing Rico's number. It was better to play the game than to get played by it. Whatever was going on at Rosa's might cause problems down the road. Whoever the men were, they had the look of settling in for the long haul all over them. Showing them who ran things right off would nip whatever disruption to the status quo they might have in mind right in the bud.

"We might have an issue," he said when the boss picked up. "Two of them, but they come as a package deal."

After filling Scar in on the strangeness he had seen, Spider tucked the phone away again and let his fingers toy with the roll of money in his pocket. He didn't like the answer he'd been given. Let Jamal check it out? Recon was his job on this patch of Rico's territory, not some upstarts the boss wanted to test. Jamal was barely worth sending out for smokes, let alone to follow the two men back to wherever they came from.

The little asshole was still trying to make his mommy proud by finishing out his senior year with a diploma for fuck's sake. Like some piece of paper was going to get him farther than Dante and Rico would in life. That, and his spray cans and the walls he couldn't just tag without some big artistic bullshit happening. The dumbass didn't have sense enough to get his head out of the clouds and stick to business. That was okay, though. He'd learn soon enough, too. All it would take was one screw-up, and Rico would stop playing nice. That was fact.

Spider stood up and straightened his jacket. What did it matter to him? He'd done his job. He had a few hours left to enjoy himself before he had to hand over his bankroll. Let Rico send whoever he wanted in to play babysitter. All that meant was less work for him.

Leaving the stool surrounded by empty wrappers and bottles where it was, Spider melted back into the night while his thumb stroked over the money tucked deep into his pocket.

CHAPTER 4

The Music Between Us

The sound Sofia Alvarez heard when she shouldered open the back door of the restaurant her husband built before he died was so foreign that it sent panic through her system. The kitchen was empty. Her daughter and grandchildren were out of sight. Sofia dropped the net bag full of produce she had picked up during her lunch break at the sewing shop where she worked. Rosa always said that seventy-year-old women shouldn't have to work, let alone help their daughters when closing time came, but they both knew it was the only way the bills got paid.

Skidding on the lettuce, Sofia grabbed the smooth metal of the prep table and used it to gain speed as she rushed to the swinging door that led to the seating area. As soon as she burst through it, ready to fight to her last breath if that was what it would take, she recognized the sound for what it was.

Laughter. There was the tinkling giggle of her granddaughter, the shrill peal of her usually quiet grandson. Wonder, of all wonders, the musical symphony of Rosa's happiness filled the room as well, and countering it all, a great, booming chuckle from a stranger who happened to be waving his fork around as he sang the praises of the pie in front of him. Even the giant of a man across from the silver-bearded fork-waver had a grin so wide that it nearly made the deep scar marring his face disappear.

Sofia stopped short. Her heart still pounded against her ribs, but now, confusion made her brain spin.

"Rosa?" Her daughter's name came out sharper than Sofia intended.

"Oh! Hello, mama," Rosa said as if everything was right in the world and Sofia wasn't struggling to keep her old knees from buckling in relief. "Come meet Mr. Bojangle and Big Mac. They have been the cause of nearly as many smiles as Dad's tamale recipe and your apple pie this evening."

Sofia saw the exact moment that Rosa set her happiness aside. She knew it was because, instead of smiling at the announcement, Sofia's brows drew together and her lips pressed into an unyielding line. As Rosa cleared her throat and said something about getting the men's to-go order ready, Sofia knew she had broken something precious. It hadn't been her intention, but seventy years and a husband gone too soon because of strangers left her wary.

Rosa dropped a kiss on her cheek as she went past and whispered, "They're okay, Mama. More than okay. They're good men. Give them a chance."

The kids were still distracted enough that they hadn't noticed the change in the air or their mother. Sofia watched as they tried to regain the two men's attention. She saw the strangers doing the best they could to preserve the joy that had filled the room only moments ago even as they acknowledged she was watching.

They looked like they had seen better days. It was Sofia's business to know clothes, to know quality cloth when she saw it. The bearded one wore things that had cost a pretty penny once upon a time. Now even the cheapest thrift store would toss them in the dumpster. The price tag on his shoes, when they were new, would have rivaled Rosa's monthly income. Now, they were worn to the point that they would be tossed out, too. The giant sitting across from him had more modest taste but just as many frayed edges and worn-out soles to contend with.

At first glance, Sofia would have guessed that all the good humor was only a distraction from the eventual knowledge that they couldn't pay their bill. Sofia wasn't a woman who went by first glances, though. She had the eyes of a hawk and the instincts to match.

"Maria, go help your mama with the dishes. Luis, I dropped a bag of groceries when I came in. Go pick it up for me, would you?" Sofia said, adding a "Now, please," before either of the kids could object.

"He gave us a really big tip," Maria said in a loud whisper when she hugged her grandma before skipping off to the kitchen with Luis in tow. "A hundred and fifty dollars! He says he's not Santa, but I think he might be in...incog...pretending he isn't for the night just so nobody wants to take his picture."

When the kids were gone, Sofia pulled up a chair at the booth and raised her eyebrow at the two men. She was old enough that not much scared her anymore, certainly not something that might harm her. Rosa and the kids were the only important people in her life. She meant to make sure that Rosa's assurance of the two strangers' goodness was on track and give a non-to-gentle warning that it better stay that way in the future.

"We meant no harm, ma'am," Big Mac said as Sofia stayed silent.

"You have a lovely family," Mr. Bojangle offered with his best smile. Cradled in its curve, Sofia saw the same unfathomable sadness that she carried in her heart since her husband's death. That changed things a bit. "They have given us a delightful greeting to our new home."

"And just where is this new home of yours?" Sofia asked. It wasn't time to trust yet, even if her instincts said that Rosa might have been right in her judgment. "You seem like the type to just be passing through if I'm honest with you."

"Not at all," Mr. Bojangle's eyes sparkled with good humor, and the corner of his mustache twitched up as if amused. "We are about to start renovations on a place that I believe you will approve of. A place where anyone can learn and grow. A place that I believe you, Sofia Alvarez, might find a dream or two sitting on a shelf just waiting for you to pick it back up."

"And what do you know about me?" Sofia asked. She knew she should feel far more wary than she did. The strangers knew her name. Somehow, instead, she found herself curious about why, instead of being afraid that they did.

"Big projects take planning and they take people," Big Mac said with an apologetic shrug. "We've done both. Nothing too invasive. Just enough to get a good feel for the place."

The sound of Rosa humming in the back room, Maria using the pots and pans as instruments as she washed the dishes, and Luis adding the swish of a broom to complete the melody floated to Sofia's ears. Something about the impromptu music felt momentous. As if a whole new world was teetering on the edge of becoming real.

"That's a beautiful tune." Mr. Bojangle's voice startled her.

"Rosa would rather be dancing to it than just swaying to the beat of her knife while she chops vegetables," Sofia said absently. "She was on stage when she went to school. More than once. And she loved every second of it. In another life, she would have taught others how to turn music into movement instead of standing over a stove all day. Maria… she would be a musician if she had her way. She dances, too, but the music wants to come out of her. Luis...”

Her voice trailed off when she realized she was talking about the people she held most dear, as if their lives were already over. That their dreams would never manifest. Her sigh was shaky when it whispered through her lips, and she felt tears stinging her eyes. How had it come to this? How could she love them with every particle of her being and believe that the gifts they were given to use in their beautiful lives were nothing more than mist quietly disappearing into the humid air of the restaurant's kitchen?

“Dance with me?” The older man's eyes sparkled as he extended his hand to Sofia. Before she could protest, he had swept her into a gentle twirl, adding a deep baritone hum to the tune coming from the kitchen. She was startled and a little uncomfortable. More from being yanked out of her thoughts than actually hitting the twirl.

Sofia began to smile. A beautiful smile followed by laughter. She hadn't done a trip around the dance floor in more years than she cared to think about. After a few laps around the make-shift dance floor, the kitchen crew came out to enjoy the festivities. A tap came to Bojangle's shoulder. “May I cut in?” Rosa asked as she set the to-go order down on the table. “I would ask Big Mac, but I'm afraid the height difference would have us tripping over each other.”

Maria came out of the kitchen and climbed up on Sofia's chair as she tugged at Mac's big hand. “Big Mac can dance with me, can't you? Luis can dance with Grandma Sofia. Then we all get to have a partner.”

“Absolutely.” Big Mac unfolded himself from the booth,

towering over the children before bowing politely to each of them.

Sofia Alvarez felt lighter than she had in years as she danced with little Luis. Big Mac twirled Maria in graceful pirouettes as she sang through her laughter. Rosa, her dear, sweet Rosa, was the graceful dancer under the spotlights of a long-ago stage once more as Mr. Bojangle led her in a waltz that carried them between tables and across the cracked linoleum of the restaurant.

When Maria's song ended, Luis did his best to mimic the courteous bows of his two new friends.

"And now it's back to reality," Rosa announced. She still wore that smile, though. "I'm afraid we need to close up for the night. Will we see you two gentlemen again?"

"Often, I think," Mr. Bojangle took her hand once more and bowed to drop a gentlemanly kiss on her fingers. "And with great joy on our part for your having us."

"Reality gets in the way of everything fun," Luis announced with a huff. "Big Mac, will you help me fix my train next time you come?"

"I will help you fix anything that needs fixing, little man," Mac agreed. "Shake on it?"

Sofia pulled Mr. Bojangle aside while everyone else was busy saying goodbye.

"You need to be who you claim to be," she said in an urgent whisper. "I won't tolerate anything less. I won't let you hold out the promise of something that you can't see through. Do you understand?"

"I do, Sofia," Mr. Bojangle said solemnly. "When you are ready to help me make dreams come alive, let me know. I'll be waiting."

"What a great night! Thank you so much." Maria burst in and threw her arms around Mr. Bojangle's waist in a tight hug. "I haven't seen Mom dance in such a long time, and we used to love music. I want to grow up to be a famous singer."

"Well, how is that going?" asked Bojangle.

"The dishes keep getting in the way," Maria said with a lopsided smile. "I'm waiting for Luis to come up with an idea to make them wash themselves. Then, I'm going to sing every song that has been waiting to be sung. I might be old by then, but not as old as Grandma Sofia. You'll listen, won't you?"

"To every one of them," Mr. Bojangle laughed. "But I hope I don't have to wait that long. Maybe you could start singing sooner?"

"Maybe," Maria shrugged. "But for now, I'd better go help Mom in the kitchen."

Mr. Bojangle wasn't ready to let reality slip in and kill the party quite yet. Humming the tune that always floated in his mind, his feet moving in a slow, graceful shuffle, he held out his hand to Maria once more. "One last dance first?"

Before anyone could object, he had Maria spinning between the tables, her laughter ringing like music.

"I believe in you," he whispered, just loud enough for Maria, but also so Sofia could hear.

Mr. Bojangle bowed out of the dance like a gentleman, while Big Mac gathered the extra meal, balancing it in one big hand.

"It's time for ol' Big Mac and me to introduce ourselves to a new friend and let you close up for the night. Thank you all for a most wonderful evening," he said as he began backing out the door. We will see you again soon."

They stepped out the door, waving at Rosa, Maria, and Luis. Just before the door closed, Bo winked conspiratorially at Sofia. To everyone's surprise, she winked back before straightening her spine and clapping her hands to signal that it was time to get back to work.

Stepping Back In

"Home sweet home," Mr. Bojangle announced when he and Big Mac arrived back at the three-story brick box that would become so much more once they had their way with it. "And look who decided to take in the stars on our stoop! That saves some trouble, doesn't it?"

"If he doesn't run when he sees us coming," Mac shook his head. "Want me to hang back? No offense, but you're a little less intimidating for most people when you come walking up on them."

"Maybe so… maybe so," Bo chuckled. "Give me a minute to introduce myself and assure Mr. Jimmy Riley that he is far from getting evicted. You don't mind?"

"I know how I come across, boss," Big Mac laughed.

"'Boss,'" Bo snorted. "As if that was anywhere close to the truth."

"Right now, someone has to be," Big Mac nodded toward Jimmy. "Better it's you than me."

Bo shook his head at the whole idea. He was no more Mac's boss than he was anyone's. He didn't plan to be Jimmy's either. The days of Robert Jangles telling people what to do were long gone. Now, he just let them know what should be done to achieve a dream and waited to see if it caught fire in their hearts too. Maybe that's how a boss should be. Mac and CJ were somewhere between friends and family. Bojangle was somewhere between a mentor and a dad. It had been just the three of them for a very long time. Now, it was time to expand the vital partnership that held them all together. Bo and Mac had taken a big step in the process at Rosa's. Now, they needed to convince the man living in their shed that he was a part of their tribe, too.

"If he bolts, you're going to have to catch him," Bo said. "We need him, Mac. He needs us. Running has to be taken off the table long enough for him to see that."

Mr. Bojangle didn't wait for an answer. He knew Mac would do what needed to be done for everyone's best interest. He knew the big man would be as gentle as possible if the need arose, too. If Bo managed his part right, it wouldn't come to that.

"Mr. Riley?" Bo called as he crossed the street, leaving Mac behind. "Mr. Jimmy Riley?"

"I'm going," the man said as he levered himself off the stoop. "No need to call the cops."

"No desire to call the cops," Bo countered. "My name is Robert Jangles. You can call me Bo or Bojangle if you like. In a minute, I'm going to call my friend Big Mac over if that's okay with you. He lives up to his name in size, but I promise you that neither of us means you any harm. We've got a business proposition for you."

"I'm not selling any of that poison," Jimmy spat on the ground. "So, if that's your angle, we can all just go our separate ways before you even ask."

"I've got the exact opposite angle to that so-called business plan as it comes," Bo held up his hands and made sure he was close enough that Jimmy could see the truth shining in his eyes without stepping into the other man's comfort zone. "We just bought this building, and before you think this is some kind of nice way to give you the boot, it's not. We want to hire you."

"You must be thinking of someone else," Jimmy said, casting his eyes down to study the cracked pavement.

"I'm sure I'm not. You are Jimmy Riley. You were a construction foreman a few years back." Bo said. He knew a lot more about the man, but focusing on the downturn in the market and Jimmy's subsequent drinking problem wasn't the right direction to go. Neither was the fact that Jimmy had lost everything, including his wife, because of it. "I checked in on some of your work while we were looking at this building. You're a solid contractor, Jimmy. We need a man like that to bring our plan to life. How about I call Big Mac over? He's holding onto a dinner from Rosa's that we want to give you if you wouldn't mind hearing us out."

"Mister, I got no clue who you are, and I'm telling you that you have the wrong guy, but if you want to try to convince me over some of Rosa's enchiladas, I'll listen." Jimmy still refused to make eye contact. Bo knew it would come in time. "Just do me a favor, okay?"

"What do you need?" Bo asked.

"If this ain't legit, just let me walk away now," Jimmy's words were strained. "I'm not looking for trouble, man. I've had my fill of it. I'll move along without bothering anybody. I swear I will."

"We're legit, Jimmy," Bo promised. "I've got nothing at all to gain by lying to you and everything to lose."

Bo waved for Mac to come over, hoping the whole time that Jimmy wouldn't take one look at his friend's size and take off running as fast as the old work boots on his feet would let him.

Mac did his best to look smaller than he was, to be his least intimidating. It wasn't easy. He knew who he was inside. Mr. Bojangle knew him, too. It was just that the mirror showed clearly enough what everyone else saw when he walked into their space. Mac wasn't ashamed of any part of who he was. He had grown far past the shameful parts of his life and become the man he had desperately needed and didn't have back then. He was proud of the changes and thankful that he had put in the work to make them happen. Sometimes, it just took other people a minute or two to see him instead of his size and scar.

Jimmy cringed as if waiting for the next bad thing when he saw Mac. Most likely, that was going to be one of the big man's fists if the world was still spinning on the same axis it had been when he woke up this morning. But, there were bags in those big hands now, and those bags smelled like the first decent meal he had eaten in weeks. He was rooted to the spot with what little hope he had left to his name. If things went south after he had a few bites, that might be something he could be okay with.

"Here you go, Mr. Riley; just like I said, a four-star meal for a four-star man!" Mr. Bojangle said, motioning for the bags to be passed to their rightful owner.

"I don't know if I'm a four-star man." Jimmy, who had been without a shower and a shave for quite some time, cringed again. That didn't keep him from taking the food and sitting back down on the step so he could try to eat it with some semblance of decorum. It was hard not to just rip in and shove as much as he could in his mouth before swallowing it whole. It had been a bad week, worse than some of the early ones when at least the bottle in his hand had dulled the rumbling of his belly. He'd given that up, though. At first, it was due to a lack of money. Now it was because he desperately wanted to climb out of the hole he had dug for himself.

"Jimmy, did you ever have a dream?" Mr. Bojangle asked softly. "If you gave up on it, you're three stars… but you can easily get back to having hope. That will make you a four-star man in my book."

"I feel like a one-star man right now," whispered Jimmy.

"Only one way to be a one-star man…and we don't talk about that. Those men aren't worth the words," Bojangle said with a gleam in his eye.

"Are you two serious about wanting some work done?" Jimmy asked once he had eaten enough to take the edge off.

"I've got some experience with being big, rough around the edges, and needing some serious work on the inside," Mac said, stepping back so he could take in the full picture of the building. "This place isn't going to fix itself any more than I could have. It needs someone who can pull out the right tools at the right time and stick with the job until it's done. The question is, do you want to be that someone? We've seen your work and know you can be. You just have to want it bad enough. Mr. Bojangle here, and me, and CJ, who you'll meet later if you decide to be a part of this, we need help, your kind of help. And what we're going to build here needs your kind of help, too. You just have to decide if you are going to give it."

"Man, you have no idea how bad I want to be that man again," Jimmy said, swallowing hard and looking up at the stars until he got himself under control again. "No idea."

"Good," Mr. Bojangle said as if everything were settled. "To start, here is an advance of five hundred on your paycheck. I'll match your last salary and beat it by thirty percent and throw in any room you want to move into, as a small bonus. We have to share the facilities for the time being, but I've got plans drawn up for apartments along with all the rest. They'll be at the back of the building on every floor. You can start on yours first if you like. The street-facing half will be a school of sorts, so keep that in mind if you don't think hours of piano practice or tap dancing might be something you want to hear drifting down the hall when you're trying to relax. Welcome home, Jimmy Riley."

"Home," Jimmy whispered, looking back over his shoulder at the big brick monster in need of an overhaul that had somehow just landed in his lap.

"As long as you want to live here," Mac said.

"I'd offer to let you stay in the shed, but I'm afraid there are plans for that space as well," Bo shrugged. "A future apartment inside is the best I can do."

"It's..." Jimmy started. He had to swallow again before he could continue. How was he supposed to put into words how grateful he was when the man beside him acted like what he was offering wasn't something out of Jimmy's wildest dreams? "It will be perfect."

"Yes," Mr. Bojangle lit up and spread his arms wide enough to encompass the future. "That is exactly what this place is going to be, Jimmy. And you are going to be a big part in making that happen."

The man with the silver beard fished around in his pocket and produced a key that he held out. Jimmy took it with grimy fingers.

"Now, I'm going to go find my recliner and get some sleep.

I'd like to start early tomorrow if you're up to it." He turned toward the door. "Lock up when you come in, if you would. If you need anything, we're on the second floor with a window overlooking what will soon become a ballfield."

"You get used to him… eventually," Mac said with a shake of his head and an easy smile before holding out his hand. When Jimmy shook it, he felt a whole new life settle into place. One that he could be proud of. "The plans are already drawn up and approved, so no hassle there. You'll need some more guys when the time comes, so if you know anyone you want to bring on board, just say the word. Mr. Bojangle is chomping at the bit for supplies to arrive, so don't be surprised if they show up before the demolition is done. You might want to keep an eye out for a good staging area when we do the walk-through tomorrow."

"I don't understand any of this, but I sure am grateful," Jimmy said.

"All you really need to understand is that Mr. Bojangle dreams big and likes it when other people do the same," Mac said. "Everything else just sort of falls into place. Like I said, you get used to it all after a while. Then, you somehow find yourself making those dreams come true. I've been where you are, worse than where you are if you want the truth. Once the good changes start rolling through, they get easier to trust. You'll do just fine."

Jimmy sat on the stoop, lost in his thoughts for a while. Whatever was going on here, everything in him screamed he wanted to be a part of it. Needed to be a part of it.

When he finally went inside, he found his way straight to the old locker room and saw everything he needed for the fresh start he was about to embark on laid out on the bench. Razor, toothbrush, soap, clean towels, a robe, and beside all of that, a stack of clothes, new tennis shoes, and a pair of steel-toed boots he couldn't have afforded back when he was working regularly.

"This is the strangest night I have had in my entire life," he said with a burst of laughter. "Dear God, if this is just a dream, don't let me wake up from it."

CHAPTER 6

A Waltz Remembered

When Sofia Alvarez was a young woman, she let herself believe in the promise that good things came to those who waited. For a while, that worked just fine. She waited patiently for love, and love arrived in the form of a boy down the street with big dreams named Carlos. Sofia fell into those dreaming days right along with him. They found a small apartment over a music store that let her teach piano when she wasn't two doors down helping the love of her life entice customers with the best food in a ten-block radius. She waited some more and was rewarded with her baby girl, Rosa, and a kind of love that she never knew possible.

In due time, her daughter grew into a beautiful woman with dreams of her own. The pursuit of them grew sticky when her heart was torn between the love of the dance and the love of a man who didn't understand it. Juan was a hard-working man, but Sofia didn't like how he seemed to rule over Rosa. Her dreams seemed unimportant, unlike how Rosa's father treated Sofia's dreams with care. She watched as her Rosa set aside her first passion to explore a life at his side. Sofia didn't like it, but Carlos reminded her that they could not stop the hard-headed daughter of Sofia. He was right.

Those dreams of dancing found themselves even more removed when Sofia's granddaughter, Maria, came along. Still, Rosa seemed happy with the choice, if not just because of the baby girl, and soon, her little brother, Luis, joined the team. Sometimes Sofia would catch a glimpse of what could have been in the graceful way Rosa's body moved to her favorite song, or when she spun in a pirouette with one of her babies in her arms. Rosa always laughed it off when Sofia would comment. She had everything she wanted and could ask for nothing more. It was a beautiful lie, but a lie all the same, and Sofia knew that deep in her heart. Why couldn't she have had it all?

The city where her dreams had come true twisted in upon itself as the years passed. It was a slow process at first. Rushed customers tapped their feet impatiently while waiting for their food instead of talking with their neighbors. Her piano students huffed and grumbled when their mothers dropped them off until they finally stopped coming at all. Carlos's big laugh fell silent in the kitchen. He started double-checking the locks on the back door and made excuses to go with Sofia when she ran errands. The city took on an off-key quality that jangled everyone's nerves.

"I just like being with my best girl," he would say, but Sofia saw the way he watched the streets as they walked.

Their neighbors moved away only to be replaced with new faces that had such a hard look about them that Sofia stared at the cracks in the sidewalk rather than risk making eye contact. These new people brought poison with them. Violence, too.

"Maybe we should find another place to live," she told Carlos one evening when she realized she hadn't seen him smile in months. Even their precious grandchildren couldn't make his eyes sparkle as they once had. His heart was heavy with worry and regret. Waiting for better days to come back around began to feel like a mistake. "Rosa said that the shop where Juan works is closing at the end of the month. So many shops are closing."

"I won't give in to them," Carlos pounded his fist on the arm of the recliner where he sat, staring into space most evenings. "If I do, they win. People like that can't be allowed to win, Sofia. They can't. We have to stay. We have to fight in our own way. We have to keep what is still here alive."

She found out later what that meant and what it would cost. By then, it was far too late.

"Juan left, Mama," Rosa choked the words out two days after her husband's job disappeared. "I got home from the market, and his things were gone. There was a note on the table that said he was sorry. What kind of husband abandons his family when things get hard?"

The kind that was a coward. It got too hard, and he knew he couldn't fight the wolves at their door. He thought he was better off on his own, and Rosa is too. Sofia thought as her lips pressed together in an angry line. She didn't say as much. She couldn't. That truth wasn't something Rosa would be able to hear yet. Instead, she and Carlos made room to bring their family home.

Rosa needed a place where she could keep her hands busy and the children close. Sofia took a job at the dress shop to make room at the restaurant. That was what you did when you loved someone. You made room for them, and you found a new way to make life work out. The extra income wouldn't hurt either.

For three months, they stuttered along, finding their feet. It wasn't easy. The pavement of the city felt like quicksand. There were never enough hours in the day to earn the money necessary to keep everything running smoothly. To compound things, Sofia overheard her husband tell some guy in the alley that they could stuff their "protection" into the dumpster right along with the rest of the trash. A chill ran up her spine when she heard the other man laugh as he walked away. She should have known then. She should have forced the issue and gone straight home to pack. Instead, she waited as she had always done. They were good people. Good things would come to them if they were patient enough.

The only thing she could be thankful for about that cold night in November was that Rosa was home with the children. They had chicken pox. Carlos was the only one left, closing down the restaurant; his refusal to pay for protection came back to haunt him.

When Sofia heard the fire trucks scream down the street, it was already too late. The restaurant was over and done with. The restaurant was set ablaze to hide what had happened inside. A message was sent to anyone who would stand up and refuse the new gangs. They fought so hard to make into a place where his neighbors could enjoy friendship and a hearty meal. It was gone. Carlos was gone.

To make matters worse, the medical examiner shifted his eyes away from her when he claimed that her beloved husband must have slipped on a greasy floor and hit his head on the stove as he fell. They must have gotten to him, too. The insurance company latched onto that idea and wrote the whole incident off as a grease fire due to a lack of proper cleaning. Never mind that the restaurant was always spotless or that the cinders reeked of gasoline. No arson investigation was called for. No crime had taken place, according to the reports. No payment was ever going to come in the mail to give some scant comfort. All that was left was an abyss.

Sofia had no time to swim in her grief. She had no time to wait anymore, and there was nothing to wait for, anyway. She and Rosa wiped the tears away before they could fall on the ink-covered pages full of attempts to find their way out of the hell that they were living in. For weeks, they looked for any workable option that would let them escape the city and start over somewhere that might still hold hope for a good future.

"I'm going to re-open the restaurant," Rosa said finally. It was almost four in the morning, less than two months after the fire. "The structure is sound. Most of the equipment still works. It's the only way. In a few years..."

But they both knew they weren't going anywhere. Not in a few years. Not in this lifetime. The only hope that remained in either of them was to put enough away to get the kids out once they were grown. If Maria and Luis escaped, that would be enough.

Sofia shook herself out of her memories and went back to work. Her eyesight wasn't what it used to be. Arthritis left her hands aching every night and slowed her steps most days.

Mr. Bojangle and Big Mac kept trying to push their way into her thoughts as she matched seams and whirred the fabric beneath the foot of the shop's only sewing machine. She didn't want them there. She especially didn't want the twinkle in the bearded man's eyes to trick her into waiting again. Not for love this time, or at least not for the kind that she once had and lost. That would never come around again for her. For him, either. Sofia knew grief like they both carried left no room for some silly romance. What she was afraid of was that the desperate longing for the beautiful world she once lived in was something that the blasted man and his giant friend were sure they could breathe life into once more. She was sure that they wanted her and Rosa, and the children to be a part of it.

He was promising to deliver dreams that were far better left to gather dust. Survival wrung enough out of a person. Deep down, she knew she had even given up hope of sending Maria and Luis out into a better world one day. There was no better place than where they were now, not that would accept them. Not really. The world was full of the same poison and violence that the gangs pushed on every street corner. It didn't matter where you went. The same danger was waiting there. It was better to keep them close and keep their heads down. They would grow out of their silly fantasies and into the people they needed to be to survive here, because she and Rosa would be here to help them learn what they needed to do to get by without losing their souls in the process.

But that twinkle still stirred something Sofia thought long dead inside her heart. There was the way that Big Mac smiled so large that it almost swallowed the horrible scar on his face. There was the way Rosa's feet moved across the floor to the music of her children's laughter the night before. Sofia was a strong woman. The city made her that way. It taught her the dangers of waiting for better and trusting in people to bring anything but pain. She just wasn't sure she was strong enough to stand up against the light of hope Mr. Bojangle brought flooding into the restaurant. And hope, in Sofia's experience, was a very dangerous thing.

CHAPTER 7

The Same Old Dance

"I think things are coming along nicely, don't you?" Mr. Bojangle asked Mac as their footsteps echoed through the empty halls of the building at the center of what they hoped would one day be a rebirth for the community. "It's early, of course, but not bad for the first day with our boots on the ground."

"We're bound to attract the wrong kind of attention before much longer," Big Mac cautioned. "Just don't set your hopes too high when it comes to a smooth ride the whole way through."

"Hope is our main weapon and our first line of defense, Mac. Make sure you are setting yours high enough," Mr. Bojangle countered without skipping a beat. "And I hope the unpleasantries show up sooner rather than later. It's always best to shove them out of the way before the real work starts. They are so much more trouble when they hover and lurk just out of sight. Don't you think?"

They made their way to what Bo very graciously referred to as their new apartment and flipped the light on to reveal two worn recliners and not much else. That was all either of them needed at this point. Just a place to get off their feet at the end of a long day, a warm blanket to chase away the chill of the night, and a view through the window of the empire that still only lived in Bojangle's mind.

It took almost a year to settle on the location, do the research, set up the plan, and put it all into careful order. Mr. Bojangle insisted that no corner be cut. He refused to waver when obstacles appeared. Hours were spent scouring for any information about the people who lived here and what part they would play in his wild dream. All of it was fueled by the profound insistence that this place would be made worthy of the people here, the people who had been ripped away or torn to pieces so many years ago.

"You should get some sleep, Mr. Bojangle," Big Mac said when Bo went to the window instead of his chair.

"You called CJ?" Bojangle asked, staring across the vacant lot into the deeper shadows beyond it.

Mac nodded, "He's arranging everything. The supplies will be here in a few days."

"Good." Bo nodded once before going to his chair. He closed his eyes, but his fingers tapped out a rhythm on the armrest. "This place, Mac... it reminds me of where you grew up."

Mac went still. "Different neighborhood. Same pain."

"We're going to make it a better place, make it what it should have been all along." There was unbendable steel in his voice when he said it, as if the transformation was already done and just waiting to be revealed. Then, his tone softened. "It's going to be a place that Sarah would be proud of. Emily and Jacob, too. I can see them here, you know. When I close my eyes, I can see them right here, Mac. Sarah would have told me my steps were all wrong when I was dancing with the indomitable Sofia Alvarez - and isn't she so much more than I expected her to be? Ah, Sarah would find that funny. She'll laugh at me in my dreams tonight for underestimating a grandmother who held her family together through everything they have been through. I think Jacob would one day grow sweet on little Maria in these halls, you know. She's such a lovely girl already, and my boy would have definitely had a crush, don't you think?"

"I bet he would have." Replied Mac, not knowing what else to say.

"Emily would probably latch herself onto Miss Rosa Martinez. It would be the cooking, of course. My Emily would have insisted on learning to cook, if only to open a gourmet restaurant for her rescue animals. She would love that the new animal shelter, where Jimmy Riley's old shack is, will be called 'Emily's House'. I wonder when the right person to run that will show up. I can't wait to meet them when they do."

Mac watched as Mr. Bojangle drifted away into his dreams. Tucking the blanket around him, careful to make sure his white beard didn't get trapped beneath it, Mac smiled sadly. It was a painful fuel for both of them, the past. It was effective, too.

Settling into his own chair, hauled up from the curbside just yesterday, Mac leaned back and pulled his blanket into place. He was used to Sarah and the kids haunting their days. If he were honest, he would have it no other way. He just wished that when he closed his eyes, their smiles would greet him like they did Mr. Bojangle. It was a beautiful world the old man visited in his sleep. Big Mac and CJ were a part of it. But they both knew that some doors were not theirs to walk through. They each had their memories to dance with and their own desire to build the world that should have been.

Big Mac listened to the night sounds, alert for any hint of danger. He and Bojangle were light sleepers. Finally, he closed his eyes. The living shadows would creep into Mr. Bojangle's light before long, but it was safe enough to sleep now, at least for a little bit.

CHAPTER 8

A Leap of Paint

Jamal "Jay" Thompson considered himself an artist, not a vandal. The distinction mattered little to the cops, but it mattered to him. His makeshift scaffold - a wobbly stack of crates - swayed as he reached up with his spray can. He was working on a design for an old building in town that he had been wanting to claim for some time. It was late, so he wouldn't get the attention of the local Five-O. They were tired of chasing him, anyway.

He had a dual purpose tonight. Rico needed somebody to follow some old guy and his scar-faced sidekick back to wherever they came from. Jay was overjoyed when that place turned out to be the exact building he had been trying to fit into his artistic endeavors all month. Sure, Rico told him to tag the brick wall as a reminder to the new squatters of who was in charge, but since he was here already, supplies in his backpack, and an itchy spray can trigger finger, why not go all out? If Rico needed some kind of justification for the time he took, Jay could always label the night as surveillance. Getting to know the enemy was important, wasn't it? Never mind that the old duffer was probably already snoring away and the big guy was probably standing guard, making sure his bearded employer didn't need his Depends changed in the wee hours. As a matter of fact, all the better for everyone. Jay could fulfill his obligations to the gang and his desire for the wall. As a bonus, nobody would have to do any running tonight.

The moon cast long shadows as Jay worked on his masterpiece. Each stroke of the spray can was precise and calculated. The rickety stack of wooden crates swayed beneath him as he stretched higher, reaching for that perfect line that existed only in his mind.

He never heard Mr. Bojangle and Mac approach. The blessing and the curse of being light sleepers was that while they might not get their full rest, they were not easy to sneak up on.

"Beautiful work."

The voice startled Jamal. The crates shifted. Then gravity took over.

The world spun, the crate splintered, and he found himself on the ground. Jamal scrambled to his feet, heart pounding. Before he could run, a massive hand gripped his shoulder. He looked up into Marcus's scarred face and froze.

"Hold still," Mr. Bojangle said softly as Jay tried to kick free from Marcus. "We need to check out that hand, looks like you cut yourself pretty good. Glass wounds can be tricky if you don't get them clean. I doubt you want to explain to the ER why you're showing up septic a week from now or how you got the cut in the first place, right?"

"If you promise not to make me come hunt you down, because you're stupid enough to take off as soon as my back is turned, I'll go get the first aid kit," Big Mac said, pointing toward the front of the building. "I'm sure Mr. Bojangle will invite you in, of course. I'm just as sure you'll rabbit if he does. So, how about everybody just sit on the front steps and make my life easier?"

"You gotta love Big Mac's common-sense way of looking at things," the bearded man shrugged. He gestured to the steps. "Shall we?"

Jay's stomach was churning from the adrenaline and the pain that was just now starting to throb from his bleeding hand. He took the clean handkerchief the old man held out and wrapped it tight around the cut as his knees collapsed beneath him and his butt hit the hard concrete of the old steps.

"Put your head between your knees, my boy," Mr. Bojangle said, patting Jay's shoulder like he was his grandpa. "It'll help put the world straight again."

By the time the big guy made it back, Jay had his wits about him again. The problem was, his curiosity was up, too. Whatever was going on here, he found himself wanting to stick around because he felt safe. So he didn't try to 'rabbit' away. They sat on the building's front steps. Mr. Bojangle was smiling like everything was right in the world. Big Mac's hulking form contorted so he could fit himself in beside the low stone rail of the stairs. The first aid kit between them was already being sorted into the necessary pieces needed to patch up the cut. Jamal's unfinished art loomed just around the corner, art interrupted.

"You've got real talent," Mr. Bojangle nodded toward the wall. "That's Basquiat influence I see there, isn't it? With a touch of Keith Haring?"
Jamal's eyes widened. "You know their work?"

"I make it my business to know about beautiful things and talented people. Art speaks truth that words can't reach." The old man's eyes twinkled. "Want to finish it? Properly this time? Without risking your neck?"

"You serious, old man?" Jay wasn't sure how or what to think. A big part of him screamed that he had fallen into some trap. Strangers didn't offer to let you spray paint across their property. They just didn't. But… what if this one did? What then?

"That's Mr. Bojangle to you," Big Mac admonished.

"Leave the boy be, Mac," Mr. Bojangle laughed. "His head is already swimming enough, I think. Besides, I am old and proud of it. A lot of people don't make it as far as I have. I think Jamal here knows that all too well, don't you?"

"How do you know my name?" That trapped feeling kicked up again, making Jay's feet want to carry him away as fast as they could go. Only the thought of Big Mac's iron grip on his neck stopped him.

"I told you, I make it my business to know about talented people who make beautiful things," Mr. Bojangle shrugged. "You don't think I would have missed you when I started looking at this place, do you? That mural you did over on 2nd Street was fantastic. I think a little more time on the river scene on 6th would have really brought it to life, but I can see how that might have proven difficult. The police reports said they chased you off a good half dozen times. I like dedication in an artist. So, do you want to get the time this new piece deserves?"

"Hold still," Mac interrupted when Jay's hand jerked away at the sting of the alcohol pad. "I need to see how bad it is before I try to flush the wound with saline. You're in luck, though. We've got adhesive stitches, so you won't have to sit through my sewing skills."

"You'd seriously just let me come paint this wall? No catch?" Jay stared hard at Mr. Bojangle, trying to see through the twinkle in those old blue eyes to whatever nasty motivation lay behind them. People always had a catch. Always. Nothing came for free, and nobody did anything out of the goodness of their heart. That wasn't how the world worked. Jay had plenty of reasons to know that.

"There's always a catch," Mr. Bojangle said with a big booming laugh. "This one is better than most, I think. Harder, maybe, but better all the same."

"What is it?" Jay asked dubiously. There were lines he wasn't willing to cross. Gang banger or not, he had his limits.

"You're going to have to choose between who you are now and who you are going to be," Mr. Bojangle said after giving him a long stare that felt like it dug through all the muck in between and went straight to Jay's soul. "You don't have to decide right now, this minute. But you do have to decide. On the one hand, you can keep inching your toes into a future that almost promises to be far too short and brutal. On the other, you can walk away from that and become the man you are meant to be; the one who creates beautiful things and brings light into this world through them. Look at this wall as a taste of the better option. See how it sits with you by the time you're finished. Figure out which future is worth fighting for because both of them promise their fair share of battles."

"They do," Big Mac said, angling his head purposefully so the ugly scar he carried was caught in the light.

"You're both just a little past crazy, aren't you?" Jay asked seriously.
"All the way to sane," Mr. Bojangle nodded. "It's a strange kind of journey, but it's worth it in the end. So, are you going to finish my wall? The job pays."

Jamal paused, stunned by the last statement. Paid to finish his wall? "There are some things I need to take care of first." Jay's brain was calculating furiously. He couldn't afford to piss Rico off. At the same time, the opportunity to put his all into his art was too good to pass up. He had to find a way to walk the line.

"I'll give you three days to sort things out," Mr. Bojangle said as Big Mac squeezed the newly cleaned and disinfected cut together gently and applied some weird patch consisting of adhesive pads and the tiniest zip ties Jay had ever seen to hold the skin in place. "We've got a lot going on here. A mural would set it all off perfectly. I'd appreciate it if you didn't make us have to come find you."

"I'll be back in three days," Jay said, making up his mind. The last thing he wanted was for a search party to tip off Rico and put an end to his chance of working on the wall. The second-to-last thing on that list was to be responsible for what would happen to the crazy old man and his big friend if Rico found out. He didn't want to push the subject. Rico was pretty good about cutting Jay some slack, most of the time, but that only went so far. He was sure the same leeway wouldn't be extended to his two new bosses, whom he kind of liked. Something about them made him feel safer than he had felt in years. He wouldn't let his comfort take him too far from reality, though. Let's see what this looked like and how he felt about it in three days.

"Call CJ," Mr. Bojangle said, looking at Mac. "Tell him we need art supplies. Professional grade. And information on which of our friends love art, and owe me a favor."

"I'll get him to deliver the scaffolding early, too," Big Mac said, like everything was completely normal.

"I gotta go," Jay shook his head as he grabbed his backpack.

"I look forward to our next meeting," Mr. Bojangle said,

holding out a hand to shake.

It was a first for Jay, that handshake. Somehow, it left him feeling legit in a way the rest of his life didn't. Like he had just come to some big business deal. Like he was someone worthy of that kind of thing, and not just a lanky, seventeen-year-old gang-banger with a love for spray cans. Jay felt his body straighten up, his head raised, and his shoulders leveled beneath the paint-stained hoodie he wore most days. He gripped Mr. Bojangle's hand like a young businessman, ready to make a deal. He was rewarded by a delighted twinkle that lit up the old man's eyes.

"Keep it clean," Big Mac said of his hand now that it was bandaged. "Watch what you do with it the next few days. I'll check it again when you come back. If you have any problems before then, come find me."

Jay nodded. He couldn't speak past a very unexpected lump in his throat. Raising the newly bandaged hand in a wave, he made an awkward exit. Still not exactly how to feel about the last half hour, he hightailed it back into the shadows down the alley.

"Things are coming together perfectly," Mr. Bojangle said to Mac, as Jamal ran out of sight, "Don't you think?"

CHAPTER 9

The Foreman's Rhythm

Jimmy Riley stood surveying his crew's work, his weathered face showing pride for the first time in years. A week ago, he'd been just another shadow on the street, hand out and hope gone. Now, freshly shaved and wearing clean work clothes, he carried himself like the foreman he used to be.

"Never thought I'd be back in charge of anything," Jimmy said to Mr. Bojangle, who stood beside him watching the progress. "Three years ago, I had six men under me. Worked on most of the buildings in this town." His voice caught. "Then the plant closed, and jobs dried up. I had to let the guys go. A few drinks turned into a lot… and, well, people aren't very forgiving of a fool these days."

"You and your men do good work," Mr. Bojangle said, spreading his arms and doing a slow circle to take in the big entry space that had once doubled as a gymnasium and cafeteria seating area for the old school. It was already coming together with only a few small details to complete before they could move on to the next part of the project. "Not just good. Excellent.. Fast, too. I had a week planned just to gut the place."

"I found a few of my old crew, they were excited to hear from me. We know how to pull together to get things done," Jimmy gestured to the men working efficiently around the building. "Jorge there was my best tile man. Mike could frame a house blindfolded. The others aren't slouches, either. And let's face it, most of us don't have much to do after normal working hours. It doesn't hurt us none to spend it here getting ahead of schedule."

"I want your actual hours, Jimmy," Mr. Bojangle said, holding up his hand when Jimmy would have argued. "You all deserve the overtime. A bonus, too. You are cutting weeks off of my schedule and bringing this place to life faster than I ever could have hoped. Just look at what you have accomplished already! I planned to make do with a few tables outside for at least another month. Now look at this place. You already have everything set up here, even though you're still installing doorknobs and light switch covers."

"Inside is better. No need to worry about the weather or pulling it all back in every night. We made sure the place was spotless," Jimmy said proudly. "Cleared every bit of glass, every hazard. Set up the workstation just like you asked - paints, brushes, spray cans, masks. Even got that industrial ladder you ordered. Checked it myself - solid as a rock."

Mr. Bojangle smiled, noting how Jimmy had arranged everything with a foreman's eye - tools grouped logically, workspace optimized, safety equipment front and center. "You haven't lost your touch."

"The guys are sealing up the back now," Jimmy felt so good about everything they were doing here. With each inch his crew won back from the neglect and decay the building had suffered, he saw Bo's dream more clearly. "The locker room is workable and can wait for an overhaul until the bigger stuff is complete and the other restrooms are available. The kitchen space won't take long. I can handle that tonight before I hit the sack since it's mostly last-minute cleaning and a coat of paint before the appliances and prep tables arrive. And you aren't paying me for that part. I mean it, Bo. I need to give something back for everything you have done for me. A few hours with a bucket of paint is small against what you have given me."

"We give to each other," Bojangle said softly. "That's how the world works best, Jimmy."

"Feels good," Jimmy admitted softly as he took in the space again. "Feels right. Having responsibility again. Having people count on me."

"They always counted on you, Jimmy. They just needed you to remember that." Bo cocked his head to the side. "Do you see how the light comes in through the big windows? I think that will make just about the most perfect spot for our budding artists, don't you? And on rainy days, the new lighting you worked a miracle on overhead will be almost as good."

Behind them, Marcus appeared with coffee and breakfast for the crew. The men gathered, talking and laughing like they were back on a proper job site. Jimmy watched them, standing a little straighter.

"What happens after this job?" he asked quietly. It was a question that had been worrying at his mind since he had stepped into the building that first night.

Mr. Bojangle's eyes twinkled. "Why, Jimmy, I believe this building needs a proper renovation. Inside and out. We need someone who knows what they're doing to oversee it. Even with all hands on deck and overtime in their pockets, we aren't going to be finished anytime soon. After that? Well, beautiful ideas always want to grow, don't they? I don't think any of you need to worry about job security from now until you retire if you decide to stay on."

Jimmy's eyes widened slightly as the meaning sank in.

"Of course," Mr. Bojangle continued, "whoever oversaw the whole thing would have to become part of the board I've already started assembling. They would need to take responsibility for keeping the construction and remodeling side of it all straight. They would need to keep a reliable crew in steady work. Handle payroll. Manage schedules. Propose new projects from time to time as we grow. Do you think you might know anybody qualified?"

"Yes, sir," he managed. He promised himself a long time ago that he was finished with tears, but right now he thought they might come anyway. Joy, this time instead of despair. "I might know just the person. I think he's just about ready for that kind of responsibility. He might just need to get the first floor finished first. Do you think that would be okay?"

"CJ will be relieved to hear that," Mr. Bojangle gave him a wink. "I'm afraid I've been running him ragged lately. He's pretty sure he knows just how amazing he is, but not so much so that he won't enjoy handing some of the moving parts to someone else."

The door opened again, and Mr. Bojangle lit up when he saw Jamal standing at the threshold.

"Ah, speaking of moving parts..." He excused himself and went to meet the young man.

"Are you ready to start work?" Gesturing at the table full of art supplies across the room, "I think we have everything you need. If not, give Mac a list and he'll get it."

"I...um..." Jay stuttered, dragging hungry eyes away from the table.

"Brought some friends." Mr. Bojangle finished for him. He smiled encouragingly at the three nervous teenagers hovering behind Jamal.

"Yeah, that's the twins, David and Ethan, and their cousin Luke. They didn't believe me," Jamal admitted. "About you being cool with us painting your place like this."

"Art needs space to breathe," the old man said. "And artists need to be safe to create it." He gestured to the equipment. "The wall is your canvas. Show me what you see."

Later, as the boys worked, Jamal climbed down to get water. Mr. Bojangle noticed his hand was wrapped up again, but bigger.

"Is your hand not healing?" he asked while making eye contact to see if Jay was going to tell the truth.

Jamal shrugged, looking down. There were so many things he didn't want to have to say out loud. So many ugly details of his life that he desperately wanted to keep those secrets from Mr. Bojangle. It didn't matter as he already knew them far better than he should. "This guy named Rico caught up with me. Says I owe him a favor. So I had to do some stuff for him. Says artists don't make money, but his crew... they always eat."

"Ah, that choice we discussed, it's coming quicker than you might think. What do you want to do?" Mr. Bojangle asked softly.

"That I'd rather paint than hurt people." Jamal's voice cracked. "It's just that sometimes...sometimes we don't get choices."

Mr. Bojangle watched the other boys working on their mural - a phoenix rising from concrete flames. "There are always choices, Jamal. And there are always people willing to help you make the right ones." He squeezed Jamal's shoulder. "You're not alone anymore."

A small spark of hope was still alive in Jamal's eyes. That look nearly broke Bo's heart. Jamal was well on his way to picking the right path.

He patted Jay's shoulder again and then went back to the umbrella-covered table beside the sidewalk, where he spent the rest of the day coaxing passers-by into taking one of the pamphlets detailing the dream that was coming to life around them.

Once the sun sank beneath the city's skyline and the boys left, Mac sat next to Bo, handing him an iced tea. "If we aren't careful, we're going to end up tripping over each other with all the new people who want to volunteer here, Mr. Bojangle. It's a good thing we have some emerging leaders from this community. That will be helpful with the projects."

"Did you find Rico?" Bojangle inquired, although he was pretty sure he already knew the answer. Mac and CJ just get things done. That loose end had been nagging at him all afternoon.

"I know where he is, and word is getting around. We are making some waves." Mac said and then sighed deeply. He wasn't looking forward to what would inevitably come next. "I suspect he'll make a move within the next few days."

Bo looked around and finished a big gulp of the iced tea. "Good, I'd love the chance to meet Mr. Rico 'Scar' Morales. It's past time he takes a good, hard look at his life."

"I wish you would let me handle that part," Big Mac said for about the hundredth time. "I don't like the idea of you being around these guys."

"Sometimes people surprise you, Mac," Bo said softly. "Sometimes, they surprise themselves. I need to be there so I can see firsthand who he is. I think there is still hope for him to turn his life around."

"I know you do, Mr. Bojangle." Mac took a drink of his tea. Mr. Bojangle had never claimed that the road ahead was going to be an easy one. Mac had never expected it to be. He just wished that there was some way to ensure his friend's safety while they made their way along it. "I know you do."

CHAPTER 10
Scar's Syncopation

Rico "Scar" Morales didn't earn his position by missing details. From his perch on the abandoned factory's fire escape, he watched his territory through eyes that had learned to see threats in the smallest changes. And lately, the changes had been anything but small.

The scar on his cheek twitched. It was a souvenir from his younger days that still haunted him. Both the mark and the nerve damage from it were reminders to keep his world in check. The thing always acted up when something was stressing him out. Losing grip on his neighborhood was doing it.

On the weed-choked asphalt below, Tyrell practiced jump shots against the crumbling wall and worn-out basket, each bounce of the basketball echoing like a clock counting down. Rico's scar twitched in time with the sound, setting him even more on edge.

"They fixed Rosa's kitchen last week," Tyrell said, his voice carefully neutral. "Old refrigerator just happened to get replaced. Jimmy's crew did the work. Word is there's some high-tech security system installed now, too."

Rico's jaw tightened. He wasn't quite ready to deal with the they Ty mentioned. Not yet. Not until he was sure that the old man and his giant of a sidekick couldn't be put to some good use for his enterprise. By all accounts, they were building some sort of community center. It was bullshit to its core. Just another oblivious white guy trying to save a world he had no way of understanding. Rico had seen the type before. They dove into schools to educate the poor, underprivileged youth they saw there. Then, they bought up all the property on some crumbling street, polished the turd they now owned until it shined like solid gold, and raised the rent so none of the people who called this city home could afford to live there.

Those grand plans always failed. Within six months - a year tops - the shine would wear off of whatever had driven the old man here in the first place. He'd start cutting corners because deep down, the idea of moving on was already fully rooted. The city was a vampire like that. It loved to suck the soul out of would-be saviors. All the new blood that got suckered into the area because someone labeled it up and coming would learn they got screwed over. The whole thing was a trap from the get-go. They would turn to Rico and his boys to ease the pain of their shattered little dreams, and the money would come flowing in like never before. The best part was that Rico wouldn't have to lift a finger for it to happen. In fact, the payoff would be higher in the long run if he kept a hands-off approach.

The problem was that hammering that point home with his boss was tricky business. Dante would see the short-term decline in Rico's market and freak out. He would see Rico's handling of the territory as a weak link in his empire. To Dante Williams, that kind of thing couldn't be tolerated. He wasn't forward-thinking enough. He was a gang-banger through and through. The money was good, but the power it brought him was better. It was the ruthlessness Dante loved. The violence. Rico was more of a businessman, or at least he liked to think so. Sure, sometimes his business required someone to be put back in line with a good roughing up. He wasn't squeamish there. He just didn't get off on it like Dante did.

His mind drifted back to the old man and his sidekick. There was something about them both that just didn't sit right. He was used to the do-gooders coming in with their fancy clothes and fancier plans. Pose for their Instagram photos and tag their sponsors. They brought their own crews with them when they came. They put more into their security systems than they did into whatever project they built. They might want the adrenaline rush and endorphin hit they got by coming here and shining up a spot, but most of that was fueled by fear. The same fear rush you get watching a scary movie or riding a roller coaster. Easy fear. Safe fear. That didn't seem to be the case this time. It jangled Rico's nerves.

Jimmy Riley - another piece that didn't fit. A month ago, the man had been scrounging the dumpsters for his dinner. Now he walked the streets with a new purpose in life. Where did that come from? Jimmy had stopped drinking. Rico knew for a fact that it wasn't because he had turned to something heavier to put the spring back in his step. A turnaround like that didn't happen overnight in the real world, yet Jimmy proved that it could.

Now, that was dangerous for business. Rico frowned, lost in his thoughts while the damned basketball thumping kept time with the twitch in his cheek.

"They're soft," Ty continued, his next shot hitting the makeshift backboard harder. Rico was sure he had missed whatever Ty said before that declaration. It didn't matter. The subject hadn't changed. Everything came back to the old man who was stirring up dust in Rico's world. "Just some church folk trying to save our souls. Probably report their good deeds to some charity board somewhere."

"Church folk don't move like that bodyguard does." Rico jumped down from his perch and grabbed the ball. As Tyrell threw his hands up, Rico spun the ball on one finger. It was a trick he picked up before he learned that talent meant nothing without opportunity. Right on the heels of that revelation, he found out that opportunity often came in ugly packages that had nothing to do with happiness. "That big guy looks like he did hard time or is straight up hood."

"So what?" Ty sneered. "Dude found Jesus squatting in his jail cell, and the shine hasn't worn off yet. It's nothing we haven't seen before."

"So everything about them is wrong. The old man dresses like he's poor, but his shoes are expensive, just worn down like he walks miles every day. He acts simple, but his eyes miss nothing. And his friend…" Rico tossed the ball back, harder than necessary. "Men like that don't guard charity workers, they mug them."

The unasked question hung in the humid air, heavy as storm clouds. Tyrell retrieved the ball but didn't shoot again.

"Dante called," Rico said finally. "Wants to know why our numbers are down."

Tyrell's shoulders tensed. Everyone knew what it meant when Dante started asking questions.

"He's not going to wait it out like I want to. And I don't need whatever shit is going to rain down on my head if I argue the point. Watch them," Rico ordered. "Everything. Where they go. Who they talk to. Find out what they're doing here."

"And if they are just trying to help?" Ty rolled his eyes and shook his head. Rico picked up the wistful tone, although it was almost as if the idiot was hopeful.

Rico touched his scar, remembering how he got it. "Nobody just helps, you stupid asshole. Everything costs something. The question is, who's going to pay the price? Ain't going to be me. You can bet today's take on that."

"Maybe it's time we shake them up a little bit?" Tyrell

suggested.

Rico didn't answer. Something in him wasn't ready to flip that switch yet. He wanted more time and a more personal view of the game that the old man was playing first. A small warning wouldn't hurt, of course. It was something to consider.

"Level one," Rico called over his shoulder as he ascended the fire escape again. "Nothing big, Ty. We just want to see the reaction."

CHAPTER 11

The Metal Pipe Minuet

The rock crashed through Mr. Bojangle's window at 2:47 AM, sending glass cascading across the worn floorboards like angry stars. Marcus moved with liquid grace as he reached for the weapon he fashioned out of a metal pipe he found in the building.

Mr. Bojangle hadn't moved from his chair. He sat in the pool of moonlight, looking almost ethereal, as if the violence couldn't touch him, even though glass shards covered his blanket and a small scattering sparkled in his beard.

"Nice arm," he shouted to the empty street, his voice carrying clearly through the broken window. "Bet that boy could pitch for the Yankees."

Big Mac's expression darkened. "That boy needs to learn respect. Let me handle this, Mr. Bojangle. If it isn't done now, it might not be a busted window next time."

"No, my friend." Bo finally stood, carefully shaking the glass away. His movements were deliberately slow, as if he were performing a quiet waltz with the shadows around him. "That boy needs to learn hope. There's a difference."

"Hope won't stop the next rock. Or worse." Big Mac knew this world inside and out. He knew the violence of it and how quickly it could turn deadly. He had lived that reality. It didn't matter that he was a different man now. This city was the same kind of cursed ground he was raised in. It had the same rules. Mr. Bojangle might refuse to live by them. He might have raised Mac above them. That didn't change anything. Sometimes, a man's stand against evil had to be hard. This was one of those times.

Bo picked up a piece of glass, studying how it caught the moonlight. "Tell me, Mac. When you changed, was it fear? Or was it someone believing you could be more?"

Big Mac touched his scar, remembering. "That was different."

"Was it?" Bo smiled gently. "Every thrown rock is a cry for help. Every act of violence raises a question waiting for an answer." He set the glass down carefully. "Our rock thrower is asking if anyone sees him, really sees him."
"So, the answer?" Mac asked.

"Not a lead pipe and a solid beating." Bojangle stared at the length of metal in Mac's hand with one eyebrow cocked. "That's what got us to this point in the first place. People want the easy way. We knew we weren't going the easy route when we came here, Marcus. Not if we wanted this place to heal. And healing here will lead to healing somewhere else. Before you know it, the whole world looks brighter. And to answer your question, the answer, my friend, is baseball."

"I'll call CJ," Marcus said, not defeated, but knowing he was wrong. His knee jerked in that old reaction kind of way. Sometimes, muscle memory ran deeper than common sense. Mr. Bojangle winked, and Mac's head was back where it should be, how it should be. He was no longer that kid. Maybe Maria hadn't been that far wrong when she insisted his old friend must be Santa paying her a mid-year visit.

CHAPTER 12

A Pitcher's Waltz

Tyrell considered himself street-smart. He had to be, to be in Rico's crew. He was getting a late start on the day, but he was out late the night before. He wasn't ready to admit how little he had accomplished with his well-aimed rock. If anything, it felt like his warning had the opposite reaction than it was meant to. Ty wasn't sure what to make of that. Old codgers weren't supposed to compliment you on your arm. They were supposed to get all wound up and start packing.

Rico was going to have to hear about it at some point. Tyrell knew better than to tell him before a better explanation came to mind. Hours spent in the shadows staring at the community center and its newly busted window hadn't helped Ty come up with one. It was a head-scratcher.

He hadn't even needed to use his carefully planned escape route. Years on the streets said he should have. The big guy with the scar should have exploded out of the place looking for a fight. It set Ty's nerves on end, wondering why he hadn't.

Now, he was walking the streets looking for an answer that didn't seem like it would appear in the light of day any more than it had under the cover of darkness.

An innate alertness to his surroundings had always been Tyrell's friend, but somehow he never saw the giant hand coming. One moment, he was cutting through the alley behind Rosa's, taking his usual shortcut. The next, that massive hand had his collar, and he found himself firmly but carefully guided through the restaurant's back door.

Mr. Bojangle sat at a corner table as if he'd been waiting. Big Mac sat Tyrell across from him in a way that took escape off the table and then slid into the seat beside him to make sure he got the point. A plate of Rosa's best empanadas steamed between them, the smell making Tyrell's stomach betray him with a growl.

"Eat," the old man said. "Then we'll talk about that magnificent pitching arm of yours."

"I don't know what you're talking about." Ty's heart hammered. His voice shook slightly, and he cursed himself for the weakness.

"Son," Bo leaned forward, those blue eyes suddenly intense, like they could see right through Tyrell's carefully constructed walls, "you can throw rocks at my window or baseballs toward your future. Your choice."

"Ain't no choice," Ty muttered, but his hand reached for an empanada anyway. "You don't know how things work here."

"I know Rico has plans for you. I know Dante's shadow hangs over this neighborhood like a dumpster fire smoke cloud. And I know you dream of something more, even if you won't admit it to yourself." Mr. Bojangle sat back, arms crossed over his chest as if daring Tyrell to argue the truth of what he had just said.

Tyrell froze mid-bite. "How did you-"

"Do you think you are the only one who watches people?" Mr. Bojangle laughed. He continued without waiting for an answer. "I know things, and I know things about things, and I know people. I know you."

"You some kind of stalker?" Ty asked, trying to make sense of it all. Not that he was a prime candidate for one of those, but you never knew for sure, did you? "One of them weirdos with a thing for…"

"Watch your mouth," Big Mac warned. He sounded almost as menacing as he did disgusted at the accusation.

"What I have a thing for is helping people find their light," Mr. Bojangle said. He looked far more amused than offended. "That requires a little bit of seeing who they are when they don't think anyone is watching. I'm an observer who likes to use what I see to bring out better actions down the road. I saw you watching the college game on your phone at Rosa's last week. You were so caught up in it, you didn't even see us come in. That says a lot considering the amount of space Big Mac takes up. You didn't notice anyone else in the room. It was just you, the game, and some loaded nachos you probably don't even remember eating. That tells me that baseball makes you feel safe. I saw how you calculated each pitch and predicted each play. That's not just interest, Tyrell. That's talent."

"Talent doesn't matter here." Ty couldn't look up from the edge of the table where his fingers were busy picking at the chipped Formica. There was a horrible, beautiful, confused pressure building up inside of him. It was hard to talk around it, hard to keep his eyes from feeling like tears were forming in the corners. He felt sick. "It never mattered here."

"Everything matters here." Mr. Bojangle's voice took on an edge. "It matters here more than it does in whatever perfect world you imagine outside this city. Every dream. Every choice. Every chucked rock or thrown pitch. The question isn't whether you have a choice. The question is whether you are brave enough to make it. You are standing with your toes over a cliff right now. You don't have time to teeter. If you don't make a decision soon, that ledge is going to give way and drag you down whether you like it or not."

"Rico won't let me just walk away." Ty inhaled a shaky

breath. "Even if I was stupid enough to believe every word you're saying, I can't just change my mind about who I am. It doesn't work that way."

"No?" Mr. Bojangle snapped, hitting the table. Even the big guy jumped a little at the sound. He wasn't used to seeing the old man come off that harsh. "Maybe Rico needs to see another way, too." He pulled something from his pocket - a baseball, worn but official. "This weekend, Saturday morning, 9 am, be at the lot behind my building. Bring your arm."

Tyrell stared at the ball, feeling its weight in his hand, when Mr. Bojangle put it there. The weight of possibility. The weight of choice.

"And Tyrell?" Mr. Bojangle's eyes twinkled once again. Any hint of temper was gone. "Next time you want my attention, try knocking on the door. Mac and I are up late, anyway."

CHAPTER 13

Silent Steps and Fastballs

The truck arrived at dawn, its diesel engine breaking the morning quiet. Rico emerged from the alley with Spider in tow. It was time he saw what was happening up close. The logo on the truck had been painted over, but Rico could tell it was pretty new, not the kind of truck that usually found its way to a neighborhood like this one. From about fifty feet away, with his arms crossed, trying to look intimidating, Rico watched as the giant that everyone called Big Mac emerged from the building. He was coming to meet the truck. They made eye contact, but Mac kept moving, not acknowledging him. Rico uncrossed his arms, realizing he was not intimidating next to Mac.

"Take notes," Rico murmured to Spider. While still one of his most dedicated lieutenants, Spider was not the man he would have chosen for this job. He hated that the man was part of his crew, if the truth was told. Spider fits in more with Dante's mindset than Rico's. Still, he had his uses, and Rico had no other choice with how things had been going lately. "It's like they're flaunting. Like this is all some kind of snub."

The truck's rear door rolled up with a metallic groan. Inside, it was packed floor to ceiling: baseball bats, gleaming with factory-fresh varnish, dozens of leather gloves that Rico knew wouldn't have a single crease in them, bags of balls, bases, pitching machines, kickballs, footballs, soccer balls, and cones. It was like a complete sports store was getting unloaded out of the back of that truck.

"Has to be stolen," Spider growled. "Nobody would…"

"Shut up and watch," Rico cut him off, his scar twitching. Even in this wasteland, what Rico saw being unloaded was too public to be stolen. Besides, that would have been beneath the old man. All it took was one look to know that. "Your idiot mouth is ruining your eyesight, Spider. I swear."

Big Mac and Jimmy directed the unloading like generals commanding their troops. Each box, each piece of equipment, had its place. The pristine, empty lot beside the big brick building had been transformed into a grid of sports equipment that must have cost more than Rico's entire operation made in a month.

"Where's he get his money?" Spider demanded. "He's doing all this right in front of your face, right in your backyard." The statement had enough venom to make Rico want to knock Spider down a few notches, give him a reason to curb his attitude. That tone would never have come out of his mouth a few weeks ago. For the first time, Rico admitted to himself that he was losing control of the situation.

Then the kids started showing up. They appeared slowly at first, cautious and disbelieving. Luis was first, dragging his sister María behind him. Then Jamal shuffled in, the first traitor that Rico was going to have to deal with if he had any hope of keeping order. He saw Rico, hesitated, then walked past with Mac's invitation.

"Come on over, Jay, grab a bag." He tried to look disinterested but failed. His painting buddies, David, Ethan, and Luke, followed. More kids joined over the next fifteen minutes, drawn by the impossible sight of new things in their forgotten corner of the world. Rico knew most of them, too. They were excited by the new stuff and paid him and Spider no mind as they ran to check out the equipment. Rico saw this as a mounting issue to be dealt with if he didn't want to feel Dante's wrath.

Tyrell showed up last, hands in his pockets, shoulders hunched against Rico's watching eyes. Big Mac jumped down out of the truck. He held out one of the new leather gloves and called to Tyrell.

"Try it," the big man said, keeping his eyes on Rico. He handed a glove to Tyrell. "And better yet, try dropping the bull and joining in, Rico." Rico's reflexes were still strong as he caught the glove that Mac tossed to him. "You might find out you are someone else entirely while you're out here."

"You'd like that," Rico sneered. He would have been forced to act if he had more than Spider with him. As it was, all he had to do right now was keep the status quo in place. This visit was for show only. It was proof that he saw what was happening and was letting it happen. "I'll pass." As he tossed the glove back towards Mac.

Rico watched Tyrell's transformation happen in slow motion. The boy slipped his hand into the glove, and suddenly he wasn't Rico's soldier anymore. He wasn't a gangster. He was just a kid, feeling the pocket, punching it like Rico remembered doing with his first glove, but that was years ago.

"This isn't normal," Rico muttered as Ty and Big Mac walked away. His voice had lost its edge. "Nobody just gives away this much without wanting a whole lot more of something back."

Spider shifted uncomfortably. "Want me to send some boys to check the merchandise later? Maybe rough up the old man a little?"

"No." Rico's response was sharper than intended. "We watch. We wait. I want to know where it's coming from. The money. The stuff. Everything. I want to know why they are here in the first place. I want to know how we can use their heavy lifting to lighten our workload and tap into those funds. I don't want them running off before I have those answers.

You got it, Spider?"

"I got it," Spider said, shifting his eyes away so Rico didn't see them scanning his face for any sign that the boss was going soft.

Tyrell was showing Jamal how to break in the glove with oil. His face lit with an expression Rico hadn't seen in years. It was the look of a kid who'd forgotten he was supposed to be tough. The look of someone remembering how to play.

Mr. Bojangle appeared then, moving through the growing crowd of children like a benevolent ghost. He carried an old, worn baseball in one hand.

"Who wants to play?" he called out, and the answering cheer echoed off the buildings like a challenge to everything Rico had built his world around.

Rosa pulled up in her car with breakfast burritos and water for everyone. Sofia was opening the trunk to get plates and napkins out.

"Is this going to be an every Saturday thing?" the older woman grumbled. Now that was more familiar to Rico. For the barest of seconds, his feet felt like they were on firmer ground. Good old Grandma Sofia got it. She knew how things were around here.

"Momma, we will be open by noon. Bo just needed some help this morning to bring a crowd. And, by the looks of things, all of our regular customers are here anyway," Rosa sang out as she danced over to the table to set things up. She wore the brightest smile Rico had ever seen on her face.

"Boss?" Spider prompted. "They got food now."

"No shit." Rico touched his scar, which was pulsing at this point. He was thinking of another time, another choice. Rosa's smile made him feel welcome. His thoughts were betraying him. He really wanted to grab that glove and have Ty throw him a fastball, but that wasn't going to happen. Rico needed to reorganize. "Spider, get on out of here. Don't say a word to Dante yet. I'll update him later."

"Will you be good without me, boss?" Spider asked as he was mean-mugging the little kids on the field.

"No, I'm good. Keep this between us till I figure out what the deal is. Don't need to spook anyone without facts. If I even think you've opened your mouth, you will be the first example I set. This craziness is going to stop." He said, trying to reassert his position of dominance. He was more trying to convince himself, because Spider wasn't altogether buying it. Spider headed out back down the alley.

The morning sun climbed higher, painting the scene in gold: children laughing, leather popping with caught balls, the clean crack of bats connecting. And through it all, Rico watched from the side. He watched all the kids, but specifically Tyrell's face, remembering what it felt like to be that young, to believe in things that came without price tags or blood debts.

"This isn't about territory. This is something else… something else entirely," Rico whispered to himself as he walked away, and for the first time in a long time, his scar didn't twitch at all.

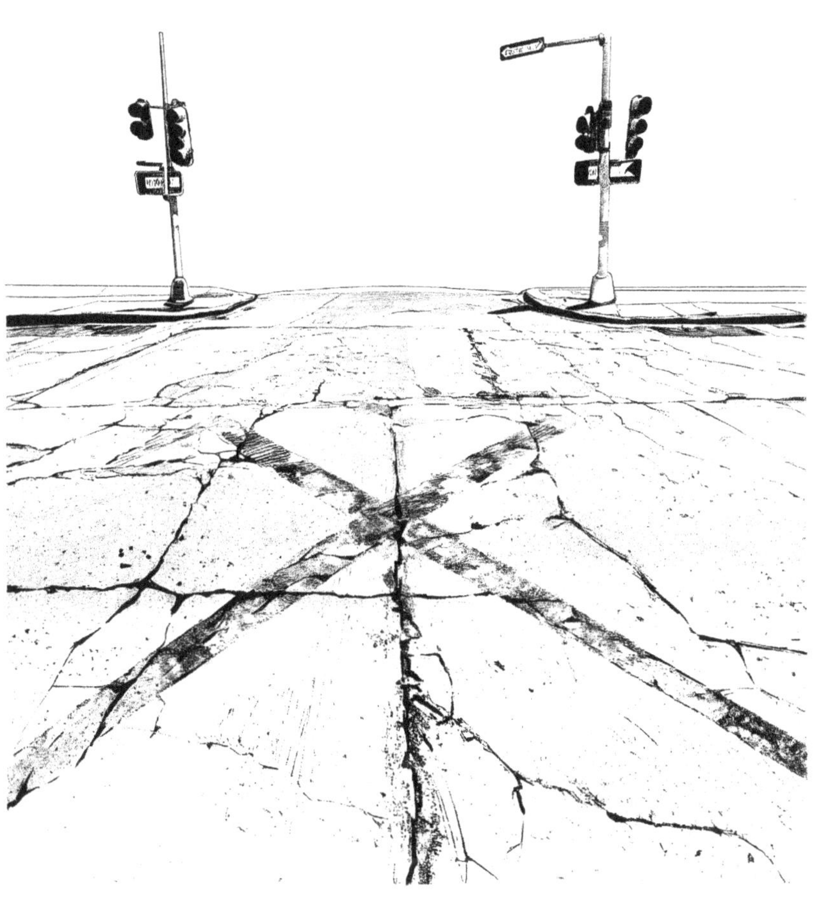

CHAPTER 14

The Dance of Choices

"Ahhhhh," Mr. Bojangle sighed contentedly when he finally settled into his battered recliner at the end of the day. "That went even better than I expected."

"We had a good turnout," Big Mac nodded. He was standing at the window, looking out into the night. As much as he wished he could share Mr. Bojangle's soft glow of contentment, he was troubled. "I kept an eye on Rico and his sidekick today. They both hung around for a while, then the little twitchy one left. Rico stuck around."

"I saw them," Bo sighed. "Rico is going to be a tough nut to crack, I'll give you that. Spider is going to do his best to be tougher."

"He's already decided which way to break," Mac said softly. "He's hungry for power, not opportunity. I'd watch my back if I were Rico. He's probably already reporting to Dante and only giving good old Scar what he wants to hear."

"We do what we can to lift up who we can," Mr. Bojangle shrugged. "It's our job to help people remember where their inner light switch is."

"Spider doesn't have one," Big Mac said. "Maybe he did once. I don't know. He likes the darkness too much now. Craves it."

"So, he's your opposite, that's what you're saying?" Mr. Bojangle asked softly.

"He's what I would have been in a few more years," Mac replied just as softly. "I wish I didn't see that, but I do."

"Then, I feel sad for him," Bo said. "That doesn't mean we

won't try to pull him back, you might be surprised. I believe we can."

"I know," Mac sighed and went to his recliner. He was tired. Keeping a watchful eye on Rico and Spider was exhausting. He was so thankful when they finally left. "I'm sorry, Mr. Bojangle."

"For what?" Bo asked, cocking his head to the side so he could study his troubled friend.

"For carrying all the doubt I carry." There was no better way to put it.

"I believe in you," Mr. Bojangle reminded him. "And you believe in yourself. Of the two, the second one is the most important. The first just helped you get there. That doubt you think bothers me, doesn't. You allow me to focus on seeing the good that can be, by keeping an eye on the bad side. I know it's there, I'm not oblivious. But you protect me from it, so I can do what I need to do. If anyone should apologize, it's me. I make you carry a heavy load. But you handle the responsibility of it all beautifully. Never apologize for seeing this world as it is, Big Mac. That is a beautiful and important job. Just don't let the 'what is' blind you to what 'could be'."

"He makes me angry," Big Mac admitted. "Angry, and sad, and frustrated."

"Where Spider is now, it should." Mr. Bojangle settled back and stared up at the ceiling. The small camping light on its rickety table cast a starburst on the ceiling. "You see too much of the old you in him. Let that go. You must see that you have come a long way. Your heart hurts for him."

"I want to punch him in the face, and then I want to pick him up and shake him until he gives it up," said Mac, shaking his large hands in the air.

"You think that would make you feel better, but that never works," answered Bojangle. "You know, there was a reason he ended up where he is. There was a choice to be made, and no one to help him. That's part of our job here. We have good blueprints. The ones that show the right direction to build a fulfilled life. Spider is going the wrong way fast. We'll figure out how to show him a better way, just like we are trying with everyone else. If he doesn't have hope, we forgive him, and we keep working at it, hoping that he'll eventually turn his life around."

"Hope is a powerful thing," Big Mac let a small smile break through the worry he felt.

"That it is, my friend. That it is," Mr. Bojangle laughed delightedly. "It's the most powerful thing we have in this life. And as long as we keep sharing it, it will keep growing stronger. This city is going to give us a good workout. That's a good thing. We'll sweat for a bit and be sore in places we forgot we had, but in the end, our hope will be bigger than your biceps. You just wait and see."

"Did I see you whirl Sofia around the table for a dance earlier?" Big Mac said.

"She needed a reminder today to have a good time," Bo laughed. "She worries. It's her way. Sometimes she is just a little too good at it. Which reminds me, how is the hunt for the grand piano going?"

"CJ told me he has a lead," Big Mac said. "If it pans out, he should be able to have it refinished, tuned, and onsite before the month is out."

"Perfect," Mr. Bojangle smiled peacefully. "Let me know if we have to go with Plan B. It won't be as good as the real thing, but I'm sure CJ will find the perfect one."

"The dance studio mirrors will be going in next week, too," Big Mac said with a yawn. "Jimmy also wants to get the old sprinkler system working, said he is waiting on a couple of parts. He wanted a little extra time on the floors before those mirrors go in. Rosa took a tour and told him the floors were beautiful, but he's convinced they need sanding again."

"He's a good man and a wonderful contractor," Mr. Bojangle said, fighting his own yawn. "If he says they need another sanding, that's just what they need."

"This is a good place we're building here, Mr. Bojangle." Mac felt his smile spread through the words. "A good place full of good people."

Bo was already snoring softly. His feet twitched in time with the steps of his dream dance. An indulgent smile twitched on his lips. He was home, wrapped in the love of his family, even if only for the next few hours. It was no wonder the shadows of the city outside didn't bother him. When they rolled in, he could retreat into the light of his most precious dreams.

Mac closed his eyes, too. He wasn't worried anymore. Tomorrow would bring what it brought. For now, the memory of today's laughter rang in his ears alongside the crack of the bat and the cheering of the crowd.

CHAPTER 15

The Crossroads Tango

It was Sunday morning, and Rico was in a foul mood. He didn't want to be where he was, and he sure as hell didn't want to deal with the reason. That didn't mean he had a choice in it either. He knew his place and his obligations. He also knew just how precarious a position he was in right now.

He had arrived at Dante's after receiving an urgent text the night before. Dante's place sat on the top floor of the Cameron Heights projects, the penthouse suite he'd claimed years ago. It was part home, part office for the drug dealer. Neither managed to look inviting on a good day. Today, the space was downright menacing.

The walls were a mix of expensive art and a couple of bullet holes. Trophy pieces taken from territory conquests sat showcased beneath overly bright fluorescents. A gold-plated Desert Eagle lay prominently on the coffee table beside stacks of cash and scattered burner phones.

The guys and girls sprawled across the couches stood in sharp contrast to Rico's memory of the day before. The men here were barely people anymore. They were hate and violence wearing human suits. Their girls weren't much better. They might be pretty on the outside, but they were as empty as the liquor bottles lining the table next to the kitchen sink. Rico had never really noticed that before. His jaw tightened at the thought of how much he didn't like this.

Rico found Dante by the big, hazy window behind his desk, a half-empty bottle of cognac in his hand. Dante Williams might run the most extensive criminal operation in three districts, but he still dressed street. He had slicked-back, jet black hair, designer clothes mixed with gold chains, and an oversized gold watch. His vintage Raiders jacket hung over the back of his seat, ready for when it was time to venture out.

"Less than three months." Dante's voice carried a distinctive rasp, the result of a garroting attempt in his younger years. He took a long pull from the bottle. "Just over two fucking months since that old man rolled in, and your territory's numbers look like shit."

He kicked a ledger across the floor. Numbers in red. Territory maps marked with X's where the gang leader felt Rico had lost control.

"We need more soldiers, and it seems you keep losing recruits." Dante snarled, pacing like a caged animal. His gold rings caught the light with each gesture. "Your territory's getting away, and you're getting soft, Rico. I hear your boys are playing baseball instead of running the product. Got some of them thinking they're artists, too. The fuck is that?"

Rico touched his scar unconsciously. Spider must be playing his cards, trying to make him look like a chump. He knew he couldn't trust his ass. "I know Dante, but the community has…"

"The community?" Dante interrupted, followed by a laugh. Dante's laugh was cold as concrete. He moved fast, street fighter fast, getting in Rico's face. "Since when do I give a shit about the community? That's not why I put you there."

Rico held his ground, but just barely. He'd seen what happened to people who showed weakness around Dante. The last guy was lucky, he was just missing teeth.

"Things are changing. Maybe we need to -" Rico started. He needed to get his point across. This was about the long term, not the short sale. Even if part of him felt a little sick when an image of everyone coming together over food and fun the day before flashed through his mind, that would be over soon enough. It always went that way. It always would.

"Need to what?" Dante grabbed him by the collar, cognac breath hot on his face. "Start a damn youth center? Is that what you think our business model is? Maybe we need to do a bake sale? This ain't some after-school special, Rico. This is business."

"Give me time. I can fix it," Rico said confidently. If Dante would just wait things out, it would all come crashing down on its own.

"Time?" Dante's hand moved to the Desert Eagle, casual but deliberate. "Nah, brother. Time's the one thing you don't got. You're losing control of your set. Fix it..." He lifted the gun and examined it in the light. "Or I fix it my way."

The threat hung in the air like gun smoke.

"We clear?" Dante's nose was pressed against his, eyes boring into Rico's soul like maggots into rotten meat.

Rico nodded, not trusting his voice.

"Good. Now get the fuck out of my house." Dante turned his back to look out the window again.

Rico didn't run even though he wanted to. He knew better than that. With every accusing eye in the place on him, he'd never make it to the door. He also didn't let out the breath he held until he was in the elevator and far enough away from Dante's domain to feel safe from the Desert Eagle. Dante wasn't above shooting a man in the back after he told him he was free to go.

For the first time in what felt like a lifetime, Rico hated the life he was trapped in. The man he worked for was a psychopath brimming with evil. Whatever shine gang life had when Rico signed on was gone. In its place was an oil slick coated in the poison his crew peddled.

"Something's got to give, man," he said to himself as he pulled up his hoodie against prying eyes.

He knew the odds of his survival if that something wasn't exactly what Dante wanted it to be.

The elevator shuddered to a stop. Rico pushed through the broken lobby doors, the weight of Dante's threats heavy on his shoulders. His car sat alone in the lot, a black Chrysler 300 with tinted windows. It was his armor against the world.

Before starting the engine, he reached for the glove box. The .38 snub nose rested there, worn smooth by years of careful handling. In his neighborhood, you didn't last long without insurance. But underneath the gun lay something else, something he hadn't looked at in a long time.

The photograph was creased and faded, but the images remained clear: A younger Rico, fourteen and full of promise, his Cardinals uniform still crisp and white. Next to him stood his father, Manuel Morales, wearing the proud smile of a man who believed in the American dream. They stood in front of Morales Market & Deli, the store his father had built from nothing but sweat and hope.

The date in the corner felt like an accusation: June 15. The next night, Rico woke to sirens and his mother's screams. The store was ash, and his father's lessons about standing up to protection rackets were dying with it.

The scouts never came back after that summer. There were no more baseball games, only lessons about power and what happens to people who don't understand how the world works.

Rico touched his scar - a gift from his first street fight, earned the week after the funeral. The same week, he learned dreams are a luxury poor kids can't afford.

He started to tuck the photo away, then stopped. Somewhere, Tyrell was throwing fastballs instead of running corners. Jamal was painting murals, and kids were remembering how to be kids.

And for the first time since he had tossed his dreams aside, Rico Morales wondered if maybe his father had been right after all.

The .38 felt heavier than usual as he closed the glove box. Choices were coming, and soon. The only question was: whose dreams would burn this time?

The Center Stage Cha-Cha

Bo dropped the letter into the slot at the post office when he picked up his mail on Monday.

"Is the game still on for Saturday, Mr. Bojangle?" Viola, the clerk behind the counter, asked, interrupting Bo's thoughts. "My kids keep asking."

"It is," Bo winked conspiratorially. "I've also got some new things arriving this week that they should check out. Your little Daisy inspired one of them."

"She's only six months old," Viola laughed.

"You're never too young, or too old, to be an inspiration," Mr. Bojangle said, adding his big booming laugh to the mix. "And she shouldn't have to spend her day trying to squirm out of your lap while her big brother and sister have all the fun. Jimmy's got a whole crew working on a baby-safe play area where parents can let their little ones work off all that energy as they watch the games."

"I don't know how you do it, Mr. Bojangle," Viola shook her head. Her bemused smile stretched so wide that it brought out both of her dimples.

"I'm barely lifting a finger," Bo admitted. He didn't need to. The more people who came to look around, the more they insisted on being a part of it all. "Everyone else is doing all the work. I'm just there to help them find the best place to use their skills."

"You know that Jasmine, AJ, and all their friends say that Saturdays are the day they visit Santa's workshop, don't you?" Viola asked. "And I have to admit, I'm starting to believe they are right."

"I might have his beard, but I'm not quite up to those standards in the belly...yet," Mr. Bojangle laughed. "Although, if Rosa keeps feeding us like she has been, it won't be long. And you make sure that you let the kids know I am so proud of them. I believe in them. They are wonderful, Viola. Great kids! And know I believe in their mom and dad, too." Bo said with a wink. "The two of you are the reason they are so incredible."

He left the post office humming as he always did. The people here were good. So good. In many ways, bringing his dream to life was far easier than he had expected.

His thoughts drifted back to the letter, or rather, to who it was being sent to. Rico was not exactly what he had expected, either. In some ways, he was far better. In others, the challenge he presented was much harder.

"So, you sent the invitation?" Big Mac asked as he pushed up from his sunny spot on the low wall beside the post office.

"I did," Mr. Bojangle nodded.

"Along with the one you asked Ty to hand deliver?" Mac grinned.

"I didn't want to risk one of them getting lost," Bo shrugged.

"You wanted the added pressure to get his curiosity riled up," Big Mac laughed. "You forget, I know your games."

"That young man's curiosity is already working overtime," Bo said knowingly. "I'm just giving it a couple of nudges, that's all."

"Rosa's?" Mac asked, letting the topic of Rico slide away.

"Of course." Bo tucked the mail into his pocket and started walking toward the restaurant. "She promised to save us some breakfast burritos. We shouldn't make those wait too long. I want to stop by the sewing shop after. Maybe see if Sofia is willing to help design the uniforms for the team. I secured a sponsor."

"And hint that it might be time for her to give up the needle and thread so she can come work at the center instead?" Mac asked.

"Oh, that's going to have to be her idea entirely," Bo shook his head and tried to look serious. "I'm sure she'll have it soon enough, but for now, the best we can do is plant the seed."

"CJ said the piano was in much better shape than he expected. The former owners weren't sure what to do with his offer to buy them a new one to replace it. They said it's just been gathering dust and taking up space since their kids grew up and moved away. In the end, they asked him to donate to the school's music department instead." Mac held the door when they reached the restaurant. One of the kids from the ball team gave him a high five on his way out and double-checked to make sure they were still having practice that evening.

"Well, that worked out beautifully, then," Bo said when they slid into their usual booth. "This world needs all the music it can get, don't you think?"

"I do," Mac agreed.

"How long do you think it will take him to show up?" Bo asked, bringing the conversation back around to Rico.

"A couple of days, maybe," Mac considered. "Three tops. The question is how many he'll bring and what he'll do when he gets there."

"We'll end practice a bit early until we know," Mr. Bojangle said thoughtfully. He hated the need for it, but would rather not risk having the kids cross paths with the danger around them. "Give everyone a little bit of a buffer."

"I still wish you'd let me talk to him alone first." It was about the hundredth time Mac had mentioned it. "It would make me feel better."

"My friend, protector though you are, I will not send you out alone. We'll be side by side when we talk to him. I promise." He saw Rosa coming with a steaming plate and instantly became his joyful self once more. "Ah, Rosa! You have outdone yourself, my dear!"

"Business has been good." She beamed a smile at both of them. "I may have to hire some help to keep up while the kids are at school."

"Talk to Jimmy the next time you come to the center," Mr. Bojangle suggested. "One of his guys has a brother who's looking for work. His name is Angel. Jimmy's got him helping out, but says Angel belongs in the kitchen, not on the kitchen. I think he might find some part-time work here, a nice balance to swinging a hammer."

"I'll do that," Rosa called over her shoulder as she hurried back to the kitchen.

"And now you're playing matchmaker, too," Mac raised his eyebrow.

"I don't know what you are talking about," Bo said with a wink. They had seen the shy smiles and lingering looks Angel gave when Rosa walked by the previous Saturday. "I'm just trying to find our dear Rosa the right kind of help around here. Anything else that might come of it is completely up to them. And the kids, of course."

"I hear you, Mr. Bojangle," Mac laughed as he claimed a burrito and dug in. "I hear you."

CHAPTER 17

Crossing the Line

Rico hadn't meant to come alone. He muttered to himself that it was a mistake as he walked on the crumbling sidewalks between his apartment and the big brick monster where the old geezer had set up shop. But something about the old man's invitation, hand delivered by Tyrell with a baseball still warm from practice, had struck a chord. Then, a second invitation slid through his mail slot. It had the same neat handwriting, the same message, the same damned politeness as the first. The hook was set, and now Rico was on his way to the net.

The empty lot behind the old man's building was quiet in the evening light. Too quiet. The whole situation made Rico jumpy. Hell, for all he knew, Dante might have set him up just to see what Rico would do. It would have been out of character, sure. Dante was more the type to go in guns blazing at the first hint of a problem.

Tyrell could be in on it all, too. Ty's smile looked genuine enough when he handed him the note. He could still be playing both sides. Then, there was Spider. Now, there was someone who could try to trap someone. Loyalty wasn't Spider's strong suit for sure. Rico should have put a hard check on his problematic lieutenant weeks ago when it first crossed his mind. If he had, he wouldn't be second-guessing now.

Maybe he had grown lazy. Maybe he'd gotten a little too comfortable with how he ran his territory and his soldiers. Rico hadn't had this many nerves jangling since the week he took over the operation. He'd proven himself then and could do it again. The thing was, he was so sick of having to.

Maybe that's why he had come here tonight. The edginess of not knowing if it was a setup by his own crew all but forced him to do it alone. Whether they were trying to defect or stab him in the back, he couldn't trust a damned one of them right now.

All because some white beard and his craggy-faced mountain of a bodyguard wanted to play save the downtrodden in his backyard. The whole thing was a mess, and Rico knew he was going to be one lucky son of a bitch to get out of it alive.

The silence throbbed in Rico's ears. He got to the meeting point. His hand moved toward the .38 at his back.

"That won't be necessary." The voice came from behind him, deep and certain.

Before Rico could turn, before he could even grip the weapon, a massive hand clamped down on his wrist. The world spun, and suddenly, he was face-down on the ground, his gun sliding across the cracked concrete, coming to a stop at a pair of worn shoes.

"Nice piece," Mr. Bojangle said mildly, picking up the weapon as if it were nothing more dangerous than a piece of trash.

Big Mac helped Rico up but kept his grip, professional and efficient, a hold that spoke of serious bodily harm. Rico touched his scar, but his fingers did nothing to calm the twitch.

"They call you Scar, don't they?" Big Mac's voice carried an edge of amusement. "For that little beauty mark?" He turned his head, letting the street light wash over the massive canyon that ran down his face, crossing his eye like a map of harder times. "Might want to work on the nickname."

"Let him go, Big Mac." Mr. Bojangle settled onto a stack of construction materials. "Rico came to talk. Didn't you? And we did invite him, after all. We need to be polite."

The massive hand released. Mac stepped back, but not far enough for Rico's liking.

"You're disrupting my business." Rico straightened his shirt, dignity warring with survival instinct. He needed to get this meeting back on his terms fast.

"No," Bojangle said softly. "I'm disrupting the man who killed your father's business. There's a difference."

Rico went still. "How did you-"

"Manuel Morales. Coached Little League when he wasn't running his store. Taught kids about baseball and life until someone decided standing up to protection money was a capital offense." Mr. Bojangle's blue eyes seemed to see right through him. "You wanted to be like him, didn't you? Before they burned his dreams to ash? Dante likes doing that, doesn't he? Or, at least, he likes sending someone else to do it for him. Is that why you are so protective of Rosa's little ones? She lost her father for the same reasons and in the same way, didn't she? Did you know by the same hand, too?"

"You don't know anything," Rico snarled, but his voice cracked traitorously.

"I know Tyrell's fastball clocks at 85 already. I know you've been watching our practices, calculating pitch speeds in your head. Old habits from when you used to help your dad coach?" A sad smile formed under Mr. Bojangle's beard.

Rico's scar burned with memory. "That life's gone. You can't just-"

"Can't just what? Give kids a chance? Show them there's

more to life than corners and cold graves?" Mr. Bojangle came closer, moving with that strange grace of his. "Your father believed in second chances. In building something real. Tell me, Rico, what are you building?"

The question hit harder than Big Mac's takedown.

"Dante ain't gonna let this happen," Rico said, but it sounded weak even to his ears.

"Dante's just another man who chose fear over hope." Mr. Bojangle stepped closer. "He's taught himself to like the rush of violence. But you're not him, Rico. You're Manuel's son. And somewhere inside, that boy who loved teaching kids to pitch is still alive."

Big Mac moved to stand beside his friend, his scarred face softened by understanding. Rico was struck by the change. Instead of weakness, Rico saw a kind of strength that refused to fail.

"We all make choices based on survival. But surviving isn't living. Trust me, I know the difference." Big Mac traced a finger across his scar before laying his hand over his heart.

"Come to the park tomorrow," Mr. Bojangle said. "Be part of what we are building. See what these kids could become with someone to guide them. Someone who knows both sides of the game."

Rico looked at his gun, still in Bojangle's hand. The old man held it out, grip first, an offer of trust that felt more dangerous than any threat.

Rico took the gun, feeling its familiar weight. His stomach churned. The cold metal felt like what it was, a poor substitute for the things he wanted to hold: a baseball, a coach's whistle, a future worth believing in.

"Next weekend." The words were out before Rico could stop them. "But no promises."

Mr. Bojangle smiled. "Hope doesn't need promises, Rico. It just needs a chance."

CHAPTER 18

Dance Again

Sleep didn't come easily for Rico that night. He lay in his apartment, staring at the ceiling, his father's photograph propped on the nightstand.

Like every problem before it, this one came down to chasing after what he wanted or taking the easy way to get his hands on what he needed. Rico hadn't given much thought to the labels when he threw his lot in with Dante. He hadn't had the strength then. His dad was dead. His mom was a wreck. Rico was just a dumb kid looking for a way to get through it all. Dante showed up, telling him all the answers. Since Rico had none of his own, he closed his eyes and jumped.

Now, it felt like he was seeing the light again for the first time since his dad went to his grave. Not the light outside, but the one in his heart that he had tried to smother when he joined Dante. Rico stared at the water-stained ceiling, knowing he had caused that fresh load of hurt to come into the world. He had to look at it now that the flicker of hope had been rekindled inside him. What he saw disgusted him.

He was terrified of what it all meant. A man couldn't walk the tightrope he felt like he was on right now if he was just going to let himself fall a few steps in. And if Rico fell now...

"I've let you down, Pops," Rico said, picking up the photo and rubbing the pad of his thumb over his father's image. "I didn't mean to, but I did. I'm everything you never wanted me to be. I want to change that. I will try, but I don't know if I can do it. I wish you were still here. I wish you could tell me what to do. I want to be your son again. I want you to be proud of me."

Rico knuckled the tears away and scrubbed his hands over his face to get rid of the trails they had left behind. Two days ago, he would have beaten the hell out of anyone who dared tell him he would be letting them leak out tonight. In the quiet darkness, the truth of those tears whispered: Hope. After so long with it, Rico felt something like hope.

He needed a plan. He could tell Dante he was gathering intel, infiltrating whatever game the old man was playing. It would buy him some time, if he were lucky. And maybe when that time ran out, Rico would have a better option in place. Maybe Mr. Bojangle and Big Mac could help him find his way out once and for all. Mac said he understood. He got out. Maybe he would let Rico use whatever map he had followed.

His dreams, when they finally came that night, were full of crack-of-the-bat echoes and his father's voice calling out from the dugout. "I'm proud of you, Rico." The tears fell even as he slept.

CHAPTER 19
The Reluctant
Partner

"I don't want that monster around my grandbabies," Sofia came over to pound her fist on the table. She had just overheard Mr. Bojangle and Big Mac talking about how to get Rico involved at the center. "I don't want that 'Scar' anywhere near them. His kind has poisoned this place, these people. Now you want him to come teach them to throw a ball? No! It's not possible! I won't allow it."

"Mama," Rosa said warningly. "Remember your promise. You said that if people came looking for a better way, you would help them find it."

"I said people, not the filth responsible for destroying this community," Sofia rounded on her daughter, fists clenched at her sides. "I have kept my promise. I have carried water to those boys who spray paint their gang name on every building in sight. I have smiled. I have handed food to the ones who throw rocks or bottles or worse through windows all along our streets."

"And you have seen the change in them," Mr. Bojangle said quietly.

"Change is only good as long as it sticks," Sofia glared at the man who had blown into their lives, carrying hopes so big that they were now doomed to fail. "There is nothing in that one's make-up for good to stick to. He's filled with shadows. He is the vampire that sucks the lifeblood out of anyone who lets him get too close. You mark my words, all of you. Rico is nothing more than a snake. He will coil up and strike at the first opportunity."

"I think if you take a closer look, you will see something very different," Mr. Bojangle said, sliding out of the booth and offering his hand. "Walk with me? We'll get a bit of fresh air and try to unravel the knot of Rico Morales."

"I have dishes to do," Sofia said, throwing up her hands.

"Give me ten minutes," Mr. Bojangle said, catching one of them gently and turning her to face him. "Mac can help with the dishes. Can't you?"

"I can," Mac agreed.

"Just right outside," Mr. Bojangle tugged at Sofia's hand coaxingly.

"Go, Mama," Rosa insisted.

"Fine," Sofia stomped toward the door. "But my mind will not change about this. About him."

"The two of you have more in common than you know," Bo said once the doors closed behind them.

"Do not compare me to that monster!" Sofia jabbed a finger into Bo's chest. "We are nothing alike."

"The same people who killed your husband killed his father," Bo sighed. He needed to be gentle here. Sofia carried as many broken parts inside her as he did. That they had both learned to keep breathing after their lives came crashing down was a miracle. "He was a boy when it happened. Nothing but a boy. He had so much potential inside him, but without his father, he was easy prey for the darker side of life. Dante took advantage of that."

"And that boy grew up to become the disease," Sofia countered. "He grew up to spread it like the plague that it is. Now look where we are."

"Yes!" Mr. Bojangle threw his arms wide. His eyes sparkled. "Look where we are, Sofia! Take a good look. Not the shadows. There will always be some of those hanging around. They let us see the light more clearly. Look at how much light has returned to the community… the people! Every smile, every laugh, every single time one of your neighbors reaches out to give, instead of pulling back to sink farther into themselves, is a win. That is happening more and more every day. I know you see that. I've heard you talk to Rosa in the kitchen. You have mentioned more than once how someone new came in or someone you hadn't seen in far too long stopped by. How they talked as if a weight was lifted off their shoulders."

"They are good people," Sofia began to pace. "They deserve to have good in their lives. They want to create more. That is a beautiful thing. But…"

"But you don't believe that a broken man who carries a pain that is like yours should be given the same chance?" Bo asked softly.

"He is too old to change his ways," Sofia grunted. "He chose his path. He is the one who decided to rot in it."

"Now, you know that isn't true," Bo shook his head. "We are old. Does that mean we can't grow? Should we just hang our heads and wither away, doing nothing to change the parts of ourselves that need changing?"

"It's different." Sofia sat down heavily on the bench.

"It is," Bo agreed. "Rico is in his twenties and trapped in a life he would not have chosen for himself, by the man who stole his dreams the same night he murdered his father. He didn't even have the strength to see how lost he was until we showed him. Now he knows. The seed has been planted. It will grow, I know it will. Rico Morales is fertile ground. Then we, all of us, need to do our part to help that seed grow. That means we don't get to hold him at arm's length and tell him to figure everything out himself. We are a part of his story, part of his dance. It's our job to help him get the steps right. That will take time and patience. And it will take every last one of us, including you, Sofia Alvarez, to make it happen."

"You ask too much," Sofia grumbled.

"Life asks for everything we have," Bo said as he sat beside her, gathering her hand into both of his. "I am just a messenger, or a crazy old man. Take your pick."

"Crazy." Sofia shook her head, but she didn't pull her hand away. "Good, but still crazy."

"I'll take that," Bo laughed. "You are a strong woman, Sofia. You have had to be. Rico will need strong people around him if he is going to make it through the muck and out the other side. Can you give him a chance? The same chance you gave to Tyrell and Jamal. That is all I am asking."

"One chance," Sofia held up a finger, her eyes steady on Bo's. "I will give him one chance to prove that he wants to be a part of something better. No more than that. And I will not have him around Rosa's babies until he proves himself."

"Fair enough," Bo agreed. "He will be practicing with the older kids, anyway." He squeezed Sofia's hand gently. "Set some of the worry aside for a while. We are all watching out for each other now. You don't have to do it all yourself."

"And what would I do if I didn't spend every minute of the day worrying?" Sofia asked with a sharp laugh.

"I am so glad you asked!" Bo wiggled his white eyebrows and grinned mischievously. "I've got just the thing, or I will have by the end of the week."

"I am never sure what to think of you," Sofia grunted, but her curiosity was piqued. "You make me so angry one minute. Next, you feel like my oldest friend."

"I probably am your oldest friend," Mr. Bojangle laughed. "How many of the others have quite so white of a beard?"

"You are a special kind of trouble," Sofia sighed. She laid her head on Bo's shoulder, and they were silent for a few minutes as they watched the crescent moon rise over the tops of the buildings around them.

"My children always used to wonder where the man in the moon went when there was only a sliver left," Bo said softly. "Sarah told them he spent those nights sleeping in the clouds."

"Carlos always told Rosa that he had gotten hungry and ate all the cheese, but not to worry. Soon enough, one of his friends would roll in another wheel of it to light up the sky," Sofia smiled at the memory. It had been a long time since she had been able to think of the man she had loved and lost so needlessly with a smile.

"I wasn't left with a family to hold together," Bo's voice had a dreamlike quality. "It took me a while to figure out I could still do something for them. I could build something for them. That way, their light would still shine. You have made sure that the brightness that Carlos carried shines in Rosa and the kids,

Sofia. It's a beautiful thing, don't you think? It means all of them are still here, making the world a better place."

"With a cranky old woman and an old man with a head full of crazy dreams to make sure it happens," Sofia laughed softly. "I'm glad you came, Bo. I'm glad you chose this place and this time. It scares me, sometimes, all that hope you keep splashing around, but I'm glad I get to see it."

"And I am glad I have a brave lady like yourself here to help it grow." Bo sighed up at the moon one last time. "Ready to go in?"

"We'd better," Sofia said, sitting up and smoothing her skirt with her hands. "Dreams are hungry things. I need to make sure Mac got the pots clean enough to cook in so we can keep them fed for another day."

CHAPTER 20

The First Swing

Rico's black Chrysler idled in the parking lot for almost an hour, watching. Rosa arrived first, carrying boxes of homemade empanadas. Sofia dropped her off with that familiar scowl, but then followed with a smile and a blown kiss.

When Tyrell arrived, his uncertain wave made Rico's chest tighten. The kid stood awkwardly by the fence, then slowly walked the lined ball field, caught between street respect and baseball dreams, not sure which version of his boss he was supposed to acknowledge.

"Quite a view from here, isn't it?" A familiar, cheerful voice asked.

Rico startled. Mr. Bojangle had appeared beside his car window like a ghost, those blue eyes twinkling with excitement.

"I'm just…" he paused. Just what? Rico wasn't sure he could answer that question. He wasn't sure what he was 'just.'

"Coming home?" Bojangle finished softly. "Time for that, don't you think?"

Rico took a deep breath and got out of the car. He followed the old man through the fence, his head down and his eyes shifting as they searched for the first hint of danger.

The bag of baseballs hit the dirt with a familiar thump. Big Mac stood behind it like a sentinel, his scarred face softened by the afternoon light and a contented smile.

"Team," Mr. Bojangle's voice carried across the field. "Many of you know Mr. Rico Morales, or think you do. What you might not know is that he's not just a new friend, he's one hell of a baseball coach. He will join Coach Jimmy today to give you all a proper workout."

The silence was deafening. Rico felt every glare and saw the mix of fear and confusion. A few parents pulled their kids closer.

"His father used to say the game teaches life," Bojangle continued loud enough for everyone to hear. He winked at Rico while he said it and tossed a ball just hard enough to catch Rico's attention. "Show them what that means."

Rico caught the pitch automatically, muscle memory from a thousand summer days kicking in with a surge of happiness and relief. The leather felt like forgiveness in his palm. It's practice time.

Out in the crowd, Mr. Bojangle was working the crowd, talking quietly to those who looked like they might leave. Rico couldn't blame them. If he were in their shoes right now, he'd go, too. Shame sat heavy on his chest. Beneath it, his heart hammered. Then, he heard the memory of his father telling him that this was his first step on the hard road to putting things right. Rico lifted his head and straightened his shoulders. He was the son of Manuel Morales, and it was way past time he started living up to that. "I got this, Dad," he said under his breath.

Time melted away. Rico moved through the familiar rhythms, adjusting Tyrell's grip, teaching Ethan the proper stance, and showing David how to track a fly ball. His father's voice seemed to echo in every instruction, every word of encouragement.

"Keep your eye on the ball!"

"Follow through!"

"That's it, just like that!"

From the corner of his eye, Rico noticed that the crowd hadn't thinned as he expected. Instead, it had grown. Not only that, everyone who watched called out encouragement. To the boys. To Jimmy. To him. Rico's chest felt tight. This time, he realized it was pride. He hadn't felt that since his dad was the one delivering the pats on the back. Now, he was doing the same for the boys on the field. It was heady stuff.

Pulling his focus back onto the team where it belonged, Rico threw himself into helping each kid find their strengths and improve their weaknesses. He and Jimmy talked like old friends, comparing notes that would be used during the next practice to strengthen the team. The kids, wild with the joy of the game, worked hard. Rico couldn't remember the last time he had been engulfed in so much pure happiness. He never wanted the feeling to end.

For three hours, he wasn't Rico the gang leader. He was just Coach, like his father before him. No territories to defend, no corners to watch, no debts to collect. Just the pure geometry of the game, the joy of seeing a kid's face light up when they got it right. He was part of a team: Coach Rico and Coach Jimmy.

Two phoenixes rising from the ashes.

CHAPTER 21

A Dangerous Rhythm

In the gathering dusk, Spider watched from behind the dumpsters, his face hard with calculation. The boss had gone soft, there was no other explanation. All that time building respect and fear, and here he was playing catch like some suburban dad.

Dante needed to know about this. More importantly, Dante needed to know who had been loyal enough to tell him.

Spider turned away from the field, from the laughter, from the dreams he'd never been invited to share. The best his daddy could manage was to leave before Spider came screaming into the world. As for his mama, well, so long as she had her fix, she was tolerable enough. Spider had been picking up what she needed almost as long as he could walk. He'd learned that the streets were better than the squat they lived in by the time he was smart enough to skip school. Nobody cared if he went there anyway, and none of the books he ignored had anything to teach him that mattered. The gang was his family. They'd looked out for him well enough over the years, and when they hadn't, Spider had learned how to look out for himself.

Spider took one last look at the field. Rico was demonstrating a curveball grip to Tyrell, both laughing at something the crazy old man said. It was like watching a man take off his armor, piece by piece, leaving himself vulnerable.

Well, Spider thought, dialing the number on his burner phone, some people had to learn that you don't survive in this world by rolling over and showing your belly.

The phone rang twice before Dante's raspy voice answered.

"This better be good." Spider liked the hard edge in Dante's demand. It was familiar. It made the world make sense again.

"Boss, you need to see this." There was no point in trying to explain what was going on.

Behind him, the crack of a bat echoed like a gunshot.

"I'd rather not waste my time," Dante growled. "Just take care of the problem. I'm sick of Rico's excuses. I want my numbers back where they're supposed to be and growing. You deliver, and I'll make sure you step up."

"What about Scar and the others?" Spider asked. He had to be sure there. Dante might not appreciate any overstepping where the crew was concerned.

"If they are part of the problem, then they asked for what they'll get," Dante said impatiently. "Now, get off my damned phone and do something useful."

Spider hung up and hunkered down to look at the scene with fresh eyes. He tuned out everything but the lay of the land and the hulking brick building.

Spider lost himself in the daydream of running the crew. Stepping up would be good. It was past due. Rico should never have been given the territory or the crew. When Spider was in charge, Dante's numbers would skyrocket. Spider could negotiate for a larger cut if he set things up right. A nice fat cash roll in his pocket would be a welcome addition.

Once he had a nice, tight grip on his little chunk of the city, there was still room to move up, wasn't there? Expansion, first. A bigger crew filled with harder soldiers. Lieutenants who he could keep on a short leash and would jump at the chance of a few crumbs to do his bidding. While they did, Spider could sit back a little. He could make new plans. And at the right time, he could put them into action and slide Dante's empire right out from under him. That would be a good day. Oh, yes, it would. With Spider in charge of the city, stupid old men and their tame muscle wouldn't dare move in and shake things up.

For a minute, Spider reconsidered the location for his plan. Rosa's place was every bit as much of a problem as this stupid ball field and the idiot community center it was attached to. A solid warning there might be a better attention-getter.

"Go big or go home," he told himself, looking back at the crowds having their nice little moment in the sunshine. "Those assholes are the source. Dante will want it gone first. After that, I can have fun putting everyone else back in their place."

When he'd seen enough, Spider tucked his hands into his pockets. The roll of cash wasn't as thick as he would have liked, but it would do for today. He had supplies to gather and a few details to iron out before he got down to work.

"It's gonna be one hell of a night," he mumbled to the empty storefronts as he made his way down the block. A feral smile crawled across his face, revealing gritted teeth. "One hell of a night!"

CHAPTER 22

Dancing in Dreams

"Ah, Sarah," Bo sighed as his dreams brought him home to the wife and children he ached for in the waking world. "We aren't dancing tonight?"

"Not just yet," she nestled in closer against him, threading her fingers with his where his hand rested on her shoulder. She pulled his arm closer around her. "I want to sit here with you for a while. The children will be along soon to steal your lap and tug at your beard. We are all so proud of you and what you are doing. You know that, don't you?"

It was a night when the dream world and reality twined around each other. Bo's sleeping mind refused to embrace either one completely. His body shifted restlessly in the ancient recliner. The part of his brain that knew Sarah was gone was warring with the part that believed that if he held her close enough, somehow she would still be in his arms when he woke.

"It's for you," Bo sighed contentedly. He was a younger man now. The same age he had been the last time he held his wife close in life. He laid his clean-shaven cheek against her silky hair. They had been so young the last time he held her like this. In Bo's dreams, they still were most nights. The children, too. Their laughter was the music that made his heart sing. "It's all for you."

"It isn't just for us, Daddy," Emily said, appearing with a puppy in her arms. She set the wiggling ball of fur on the ground and walked closer. Each step transformed her from the sweet twelve-year-old child she had been on the last day of her life to the woman she never had the chance to become. "It's for everyone." The beautiful woman who looked so much like her mother at the same age sat beside her parents. "The Center you are building and the people you are building it with are just the start. You'll see."

A young man joined them. Bo recognized the same determined smile that eight-year-old Jacob wore every day of his young life. Bo lost his breath, both in the dream and in the real world.

"You are so tall," Bo whispered as Jacob rolled out a set of blueprints on a table that appeared beside him. "Sarah, look at our beautiful children. Look how they have grown." Tears rolled down his face as he couldn't help but just touch their faces. Sarah smiled back knowingly.

"Look how you have grown," Sarah said as she touched his beard, which was now in the dream world. Silver threaded through her hair now, too. She reached up and moved the glasses she hadn't needed in her younger years to the top of her head, revealing the laugh lines at the edges of her eyes. "Youth is beautiful while it lasts, but we all deserve to grow into who we were meant to be."

"I'm sorry you didn't get that chance," Bo's voice choked on the truth that hovered over this reunion. "I'm so sorry."

"Now, now," Sarah said, reaching up to cup his now-bearded face. "None of that."

"We're here to celebrate with you," Emily nudged his shoulder with hers.

"And to let you see that because of what you are building here, others will have a solid starting point to add more to it," Jacob held up the blueprints, where faint new lines had appeared. "Do you see this one?"
"That is a veterinary clinic just now forming in the dreams of a little girl two streets over," Emily's eyes shone as her

delicate finger traced over the faint image. "And this one -"

"Stop hogging the spotlight, Em," Jacob said, brushing her hand away playfully. "That is a small engineering school. It will be all hands-on learning. One of Jimmy's crew has been scribbling notes about it for weeks now."

"And this one," Sarah said, pulling Bo up and turning him around. The bench disappeared beneath him. His family stood on the top step of the brick building now, with the crumbling apartments across the street newly transformed into so much more. "This is destined to become a new home for senior citizens. They will get the care they need when they need it, and the safety they need as well. But the real magic will be that everyone who lives here will still be a vital part of the community. They will be able to hand down the knowledge gathered over their lifetimes by teaching the younger generations. There will be a gigantic community garden project next door." The garden magically appeared before Bo's eyes as her hand swept over the blueprints.

"And a park down the street," Jacob pointed out. Suddenly, what had been a slumping relic left to rot was replaced by grass, trees, a walking path, and a central playground.

"Don't forget the rest," Emily laughed, spreading her arms wide and spinning. As she did, her giggles made the happy tears flow even more from Bo's eyes. All around, there appeared a vibrant quilt of shops, apartments, and people. Smiling, friendly people who took the time to talk to their neighbors, a community that was thriving and growing.

"There will be bumps in the road," Sarah said, suddenly becoming serious. "You need to be ready for them, honey. And you need to remember what is important. Hope. You hold on tight to that, Bo. You hold on to it no matter what happens, okay? Promise me."

"I hate this part," Emily sighed as clouds rolled into the dream, casting shadows over the sunny streets.

"Me too." Jacob rolled up the blueprints in his hands and shook his head.

Something nagged at Bo as the dream began to fade into smoke.

"I promise, Sarah. I promise. Don't go," he said, catching Sarah's hand. "Please… don't go."

The smoke drifted in the shadows, making them more ominous.

"It's going to be okay, my love." Sarah touched his cheek and kissed him on his forehead, a sad smile creasing the crow's feet at the corners of her eyes. "Hold on to your hope. Believe that this is only a bump in the road. Help everyone else do that, too. If you do, I promise you, every beautiful thing you can imagine is just up ahead."

Jacob's big hand clamped down on his dad's shoulder. His body shook with the force of it. "Dad, we have to go. Wake up, we have to go," Jacob repeated as his family faded into the clouds of smoky darkness that enveloped the dream.

"Don't go!" Bo called out one last time.

"We have to," Big Mac insisted. "Mr. Bojangle. We have to go now!"

"Mac?" Bo came fully awake as his friend's face appeared where his son's just was. Bo came to, only to discover that the hand shaking him was Mac's. The nightmare had followed him. Smoke filled the room, sending him into a coughing fit.

"Come on, Mr. Bojangle," Big Mac pulled Bo up from the chair and pushed him toward the door. "There's no time. We have to go. The Center is on fire."

"How? Why?" Bo's eyes stung with tears. His heart ached as those tears rolled down his old cheeks to catch in his beard.

"We'll find out," Mac said as he rushed them both through the chaos. "Don't worry about that right now."

Flames danced through the smoke in too many places to count as Mr. Bojangle and Big Mac made their way through the smoke. A lake of fire on the newly finished dance floor reflected in the tall mirrors on the far side of the room. Artists' easels toppled as the flames devoured their legs, sending landscapes and still-lifes to join the inferno. The kitchen was nothing more than a swirling ball of fire that licked greedily at the walls of the first floor as they ran for the doors. The last sound Bo heard before the doors crashed closed behind them was the discordant sound of the piano he hadn't even been able to show Sofia yet, crashing in on itself as the fire claimed it.

"You can't go back inside," Mac caught Bo firmly when he tried to rush back in, after they reached safety. "I will put you over my shoulder and carry you all the way to CJ's office if you even try. Do you hear me? Do you understand me, Mr. Bojangle?" The tone that Mac spoke was one rarely heard. Bojangle, usually cavalier in his replies as the elder statesman, knew better than to test him.

"I hear you, Mac." Bo's knees buckled, and he knelt on the pavement, failing to fight the tears back. Somewhere in the distance, he could hear fire trucks screaming their way through the streets. The sound they made was nothing compared to the anguished cry in his heart. "I'm sorry, Sarah… I'm so sorry." He said to himself as he slumped forward on the ground.

"We'll get through this," Big Mac lowered himself to the ground beside Mr. Bojangle. "I promise you, Mr. Bojangle. We'll get through this. It's just a bump in the road."

"It's just a bump in the road? That's what Sarah said in my dream," Bo took a shaky breath. "We have to hold on to our hope. We have to believe even harder that we can do this. They will be looking at us. They will need us. Sarah was right. It's just a bump."

"We'll do that," Big Mac said softly. "We'll all do that. Don't you worry."

Bo did his best, but as the smoke curled in billowing clouds from the windows and the flames danced on his second most precious dream, his tears cut rivers through the soot on his face and in his beard. Beside him, Big Mac sat strong for both of them even as he choked down the growing lump in his throat.

"Wait," Mr. Bojangle said with sudden urgency. "Where is Jimmy? He should be back from the errands I sent him on earlier. He should have been back hours ago."

They were both on their feet in a flash.

"Go around," Bo ordered, pointing to the left as he turned right. "We've got to find him."

Ashes on the Dance Floor

An ugly black column of smoke rose against the evening sky like an accusing finger. Rico's foot hit the gas before his mind fully processed what it meant. By the time his Chrysler skidded into the lot, the flames had already claimed half the building where Mr. Bojangle had made his home.

The sports complex storage room was an inferno. Through the flames, Rico could see baseballs melting, bats turning to ash, and gloves curling like dying things.

Jimmy Riley's pickup truck sat cockeyed near the entrance, driver's door flung wide, engine still running. His old hard hat lay on the seat where he'd tossed it after loading the bed of the truck with used brick from a demo on the other side of the park.

"Jimmy!" Big Mac's voice carried over the roar of the flames, over the distant wail of sirens.

The icy chill that ran up Rico's spine spurred him into action. He ran as close as he could to the sports center, begging the universe that he would not see Jimmy Riley there. Skidding to a halt, he saw the side door that led into the main body of the brick building standing wide open, flames pouring out of it like a living nightmare. He knew. Deep down, he knew that Jimmy had gone inside. His stomach lurched like someone had punched him in the gut.

"JIMMY!" yelled Mr. Bojangle.

"Jimmy, where are you?" Rico's shout joined the search. He didn't need to waste time asking questions or waiting for answers. All he needed was to find his friend and make sure he was okay. He had to be. The firestorm was consuming everything inside the brick walls.

A crash answered from inside. Through windows already black with smoke, they caught movement, a familiar silhouette stumbling deeper into the building. Jimmy Riley, the man who'd gone from begging on corners to leading a crew, was fighting his way through hell itself.

"We need to go get him out," Rico yelled, recognition hitting him like a punch. "Why isn't he already out?"

In his heart, Rico knew the answer already. The Center was on fire. Jimmy wasn't the type of man who could just let it burn. This place had saved him. He was going to save it back. Jimmy ran in to get the sprinkler system to work.

A young man in a baseball jersey ran past them towards the fire. "COACH JIMMY!" yelled Tyrell.

"You can't," Rico caught Ty in a bear hug and pulled him back. Mac helped secure Ty.

"Let me go," Tyrell fought hard to get away. If he could just get inside, maybe he could beat the flames back enough to find Jimmy.

"You'll die before you ever find him through that smoke," Mr. Bojangle put his old hands on Ty's cheeks and forced him to look at him as he spoke. Tyrell could see the truth in his devastated blue eyes.

"If I can just get him out," Tyrell started sobbing. "It will be more than enough. I don't care what happens to me."

"But Jimmy does," Mr. Bojangle said softly. "I do. Big Mac does. Rico does. You have so many people who need you. Jimmy would want you to be safe, too."

The crowd grew as people ran toward the flames. They carried buckets of water or sand. Anything that could be used to smother the blaze. Each one did their best to keep the fire from spreading. Jamal moved his spray cans back from the wall. The fresh paint was still wet on the mural he'd worked on earlier that evening.

When they could do no more, the crowd stepped back to stand vigil. Maria clutched Luis, both of them crying as they leaned against their mother. Sofia's eyes held unshed tears, but her lips' tight line spoke more of anger than despair. Tyrell stood frozen in fear of what he was watching.

A section of the roof collapsed with a sound like damnation. But through a window on the second floor, they saw him. Jimmy Riley, silhouetted against the flames. He pulled himself up to the window frame, coughing and gasping. He was clutching something to his chest. It was his coach's hat. He held it over his heart, like in a salute of honor. For one moment, one heartbeat, he looked down at them all… and he smiled.

Everything went slow and quiet for a moment. They all saw his smile. It wasn't a scared smile. It wasn't a goodbye smile. It was the smile of a man who'd found life again, found his worth again. A man who made an impact, and a man who'd rather die trying to save something good than live with its loss. He looked around at the neighbors and friends he had loved, and he gave a thumbs up! It was the smile of a man that fixed the sprinkler system. You could hear the hissing from the snake-like fire as the water started showering down behind him.

Then, the world came down in flames and thunder.

The crash brought everyone to their knees. Sparks flew like angry stars. Big Mac and Rico had to physically restrain Tyrell from running in. The boy fought like a wild thing, screaming for Jimmy, fighting for everything he was worth, for the hope that was dying in front of them. Mac and Rico cried out as they took the young man to the ground in slow motion. They all knew Jimmy was gone.

Rico pulled Ty into his arms and held him tightly as they both cried. When Jamal came over, the three of them huddled together, holding each other up even though the new foundation they had found had turned to ash.

"We can't go back, man," Ty dug his fingers into the arms around him. "I won't go back. That would mean Jimmy died for nothing."

"We won't let that happen," Jamal insisted. "We can't let that happen."

"We won't," Rico agreed. "Jimmy deserves better, and that's what we're going to give him."

When the fire trucks finally arrived, they fought their way through the remaining blaze. It took some time, but under the partially collapsed roof, they found Jimmy near the window. He'd wrapped his old work jacket around his coach's hat, trying to protect it, and what it represented to him. The chance to be more than what the streets said you could be. The chance to be a four-star man.

In his pocket, they found two pictures. The first was Jimmy with his old construction crew, taken on the day they finished a major construction project. The second was of Jimmy with his kids on the baseball field. On the back, in fresh ink, he'd written: "My kids."

The fire was nothing more than a few hot spots now, but even as the last ember died, something else was igniting. The people, the dreamers, the kids, the parents…all of them wanted revenge. They looked to Bojangle and Mac, and now Rico, for leadership.

CHAPTER 24

A Pause Between Steps

The fire left more than ash - it left questions. Quickly, the question of housing was answered. Rosa set to work on a space above the restaurant for Bo and Mac. Rosa's was the perfect place to gather over the next few days and discuss the next steps.

The usual whispered questions were floating around. Everyone knew that the fire wasn't an accident. They knew faulty wiring wasn't to blame. Rico didn't have any doubts about what happened.

"Spider," he said quietly to Mr. Bojangle, "He's been making moves, watching, trying to prove himself to Dante. So he was most likely the guy. Dante gave him the go-ahead. This has his stink all over it. He's high up enough now, though, that he doesn't get his hands dirty with the ashes."

Mr. Bojangle nodded but kept his eyes on Tyrell, who hadn't moved from the seat in Jimmy's truck. The boy stared at the smoldering ruins and held Jimmy's cap.

Rico recognized the look settling into Ty's eyes. He'd seen it in the mirror, the day after his father's store burned. That dangerous calcification of hope into hatred sent a chill skittering up Rico's spine.

"Mr. Bojangle," Rico knew he had to do something before Ty was lost. "Tyrell's not ok."

"I know. He is going to need every last one of us to get him through this loss. Go hang with him tonight, Rico." Mr. Bojangle looked over at Mac. "You go too. I'll be fine. Ty needs you both. He needs Rico to meet him where he is. Mac can help pull him through to the other side, because he's already finished that part of his journey. Ty needs to know that it's okay to feel the now, but he needs to have hope that there is better up ahead. You two, don't let him get a scar, too."

"Not to take away from Ty's," Rico cleared his throat, "but I could use a solid reminder right now, too."

"You got it," Mac agreed. "I'll connect with CJ for an update before we go. Maybe see if he's got time for a video call too. He's got just as much to say about getting through as I do."

"I'll see if Jamal can bring dinner," Mr. Bojangle said. "Ty's mom shouldn't have to take on feeding all of you, and I know that Jamal, Rosa, and the others could use something constructive to do right about now."

"My uncle can store Jimmy's truck," Rico said with another wary look at Tyrell. "I don't think it's good to leave it here. Maybe later, we can use it for the team or something, or maybe give it to Ty. That probably sounds stupid."

"I don't think that sounds stupid at all," Mr. Bojangle smiled, and the hint of a twinkle lit in his eye for the first time all day. "I think Jimmy would love the idea."

"I won't say anything to Ty about it yet," Rico said, "Not until he's ready. For now, I'd better go talk him into sitting with his former gang leader, while we try to save him over tacos and empanadas. I'll see you tomorrow, Mr. Bojangle."

"You will," Bo assured him. He reached over and squeezed Rico's shoulder. "Tomorrow is another day, Rico. It's another chance to win; that is exactly what we will do. Remember that I believe in you."

"For what it's worth, I believe in you, too, Mr. Bojangle," Rico said solemnly.

"That, my friend, is worth far more than gold," Bo turned back toward what was left of the center he had put so much of his heart into. He felt lighter somehow. More determined. More doggedly hopeful. "Thank you, Sarah. I love you," he whispered to himself as he slowly walked through the few remaining neighbors.

The crowd had dispersed slowly, like mourners reluctant to leave a grave. But darkness held its own dangers in their neighborhood tonight, and even grief had to bow to survival. The last one to leave was Mac, who waited out of sight and followed at a distance to make sure that Mr. Bojangle made it safely back to Rosa's before heading to join Rico.

CHAPTER 25

A Dance in the Dark

The knock came just before midnight. Sofia stood in Bo's temporary doorway. She wanted, no, needed, to catch him away from everyone else. Her face was carved with shadows and something harder than anger.

"Where does it come from?" Her voice was steel, blanketed in exhaustion. "The equipment, the construction supplies, the payroll. Who are you? I'm not leaving until I get answers."

"Come in, Sofia." Bo gestured to a chair, but she remained standing.

"You sweep in here like some fairy godfather, throwing around money and dreams like candy." Her aching hands trembled. "But dreams don't pay bills. Dreams don't change reality. You know what the reality is, Bo? Jimmy is dead. Tyrell will never make the majors. Jamal won't get into art school. Maria..." Her voice caught. "Maria will end up serving tables like her mother. She'll measure her hours between two jobs and a broken family like I do. Luis will put his hands to use tightening bolts, probably in some damned chop shop! All while the part of him that holds so many ideas withers away. They will settle for what is here for them and make the best life they can."

Mr. Bojangle leaned against the back of a spare dining room chair that Rosa had brought up earlier. That, a small table, and two makeshift beds on the far side of the little room, made for a comfortable short-term living arrangement. The space was spotless and smelled of pine cleaner. The sheets were crisp, the blankets soft and warm. It was far more than he required to be content, and he was grateful for it all. "Like you did… instead of teaching music?"

The words hit her like a physical blow. "How dare you?"

"The way you watch Maria when she sings. The way your fingers move following phantom keys. The way you hum when you think no one's listening." Bo pushed each point home as gently as possible, but he left no option for Sofia to avoid them. "As for how I dare, hope is a daring thing. We have to be up for whatever it demands of us. We have to overcome all the doubts if we let it into our lives."

"Hope is dangerous," she whispered, but her voice wavered. "Hope makes promises it can't keep."

"No, Sofia." He moved closer and held out his hand like he had that first day to Rosa. "Hope doesn't promise anything. Hope opens doors. We choose whether to walk through them."

"And when those doors slam shut? When your husband dies, and nobody will call it the murder that you know it was? When the monsters who killed him pay no price for their actions? When the insurance company screws you?" Rosa's voice was fighting the tears, choked with the pain of the past. "When your daughter's husband walks out? When she works her fingers to the bone, day in and day out, to keep her children fed and a roof over their heads? Or how about you? When your money is gone? When you have no choice but to leave this place if you want any sort of life at all? What then?" The first tear fell, then another. "I couldn't save them. Couldn't save myself. Everything I believed in..."

"Dance with me," Bo said softly.

"What?" Sofia laughed in disbelief. "That is all you have? Is that your answer? Do you not see the world coming apart around us all?"

"Dance with me, Sofia Alvarez. In the darkest moments, a

dance can lift your spirit." Bo knew what fear looked like and how desperation tasted. He had stared into that abyss for far too long after Sarah and the kids were gone. Most importantly, he knew beyond the shadow of a doubt that there was a way to step away from all that darkness and back into the light because he had lived that part of his story, too.

He started humming Rosa's song from the first night he met them. Almost against her will, Sofia took his hand.

"I taught Rosa that song," she whispered on a shaky breath as Bo led her in a gentle waltz. His voice carried warmth like a forgotten summer. She felt it melting the glacier that was grinding her soul away inside her.

"Hope breeds possibilities. Every child who picks up a baseball, every song Maria sings, every painting Jamal creates, every child Rico coaches, every pitch Tyrell throws - they're not just dreaming. They're becoming." Bo cradled Sofia's hand in his as their feet found the steps of the waltz on the old floorboards. Luis's dream is still forming, but one day, he will make it a reality. We just have to give them all the light they need to make that happen. We need to be their light when they can't find it alone. Do you understand, Sofia?"

Sofia's tears flowed freely now. "I'm so tired of being strong, of being practical. Of killing their dreams to protect them from disappointment."

"Then stop." He danced her toward the window, where the moon painted silver lines across the neighborhood. "Be brave instead. Brave enough to believe again."

Bo spun her out to where only their fingers were still touching and did a little step dance that made her grin. The music played on in her head, and Sofia heard echoes of the girl she'd been, the teacher she'd wanted to become. Suddenly, that girl didn't feel like a stranger anymore.

"I believe in you," Mr. Bojangle whispered, and for one shining moment, Sofia believed too.

Sofia started downstairs to her family's home, feeling strangely optimistic. Although none of her questions were answered, she still felt like everything would be just fine. The storm was still inside her, the glacier still threatening to press its icy coldness into any soft spot it could find, but dancing with Bo made those threats feel small. Controllable. Nothing more than a lingering annoyance hovering somewhere at the edge of Sofia's thoughts. What she felt was hope, even in the storm. She wrapped it around herself like a warm blanket, like a life preserver. In its warmth, Sofia Alvarez understood that this kind of hope was all she had ever wanted and all she needed to get her through.

CHAPTER 26

Stepping In

The following day, Mr. Bojangle invited everyone in the neighborhood to a meeting at Rosa's that evening. They came and brought others with them. Rosa's little restaurant never felt smaller. People packed every corner, mothers with worry lines etched deep, fathers with hands clenched in fists, Jimmy Riley's crew standing like sentinels along the back wall. Jamal and his artists huddled near the window, their faces still smudged with ash from a day spent trying to salvage anything that might be the key to a new start at the center.

Big Mac and Mr. Bojangle sat at that same table where it all began, where two strangers had first cracked open this neighborhood.

Rico stood beside Tyrell as they waited for the old man to address his gathered family.

"Everyone," Bo began softly, "I know things seem scary right now."

The door chime cut through his words, followed by a slamming of it against the wall. The shock brought them to an end before they even began.

Dante Williams entered like spilled oil, toxic and spreading. His enforcers flanked him, hardware poorly concealed beneath designer jackets. Spider skulked behind them, smirking with satisfaction.

"Quite a gathering." Dante's smile was all predator, no warmth. "Hope you don't mind if we join this… community discussion?"

The silence felt like held breath. Even the children were still.

Mr. Bojangle stepped forward, and his gentle movement made Dante's entourage look insignificant. "We've been expecting you, Mr. Williams. Come in, there's nothing to be afraid of."

"Afraid?" Dante's laugh was sharp as broken glass. "Old man, you don't know what fear is. Not yet. But you will."

"No." Mr. Bojangle's voice carried that strange ancient wisdom, and his eyes twinkled, although this time it wasn't with delight but with certainty. "I know fear intimately. I've danced with it. I've seen it wear many faces. Yours is pretty generic when it comes right down to brass tacks. The scary drug dealer? I've seen far, far worse. Then again, nothing scares me anymore. I've learned to live through the dark days. To live with my ghosts and my losses. And I have learned that the only way forward is through. I'm offering you a chance, Dante. A chance at far better than what you've woven around yourself, will you take it?"

Mr. Bojangle extended his hand, an offer of peace that made Dante's enforcers shift uncomfortably. Spider peered between them, looking confused. This wasn't how this meeting was supposed to go. His eyes shifted to Dante. If the gang leader was stupid enough to shake the old idiot's hand, Spider would lose his mind here and now.

"You're either bat shit crazy or you've got a death wish," Dante spat. "This meeting isn't yours to run anymore, it's mine. Just like this city is mine. Now, sit your ass down."

Big Mack shifted in his seat. He needed to be in a better position to protect Mr. Bojangle if it came to it, and by all appearances, that moment was inevitable.

"Let's grab some dinner," Bo said reasonably. "Let these people go home. Then you and I can discuss anything you like."

"Fuck you, old man." Dante's facade cracked slightly. "You don't know shit. We talk right here. Right now. And everybody stupid enough to show up is going to get comfortable and listen to how things are going to be from now on. Playtime is over. I'm getting my territory back under control."

"Nobody wants this, Dante." Rico stepped forward, his voice steady.

"Stay out of this, Rico." Dante's hand trembled slightly. "You're already dead. I just haven't bothered putting your bitch ass down yet. Your turn's coming."

"Why is having dreams a betrayal?" Rico demanded. "And a betrayal of what? The shit life you are clinging to? The poison you push? If I'm going to an early grave, it's going to be because I want better, not because I'm holding on by my fingernails to a life that ain't worth living."

"SHUT UP!" The gold-plated gun appeared like a magic trick gone wrong.

"These people are building something beautiful," Mr. Bojangle said quietly. "But you? You're still playing with matches, trying to burn away the pain."

The Desert Eagle moved away from Rico to aim at Bojangle's heart. Rico edged closer to Mr. Bojangle, his eyes never leaving Dante's. There was no way he was going to let evil win today.

"No more death," Bo continued calmly. "No more fathers lost. No more dreams burned to the ground. It ends here,

Dante. It ends now. One way or another."

"You're right about that." Dante's gun twitched toward Rico again. "You chose the wrong path, traitor. Here's your prize."

The shot cracked with the sharp sound of summer lightning. The boom was deafening. Time stretched slowly like taffy. The blast echoed, continuing in a moment of frozen time. Rico winced as he stepped back. He waited for the pain to kick in from wherever the bullet pierced him. He wasn't scared anymore. If it was his time to die, he would die for his kiddoes. He would die as Coach Rico, the son of Manuel 'Manny' Morales. He would die proud.

Everyone was rushing, screaming, trying to get away or to rush at Dante and his crew with vengeance in their eyes. Big Mac pushed Luis out of the way and fell to his knees in front of the booth, his back to the room, his body stretching to fill even the smallest gap between the kids and Dante.

It was all happening in an instant, even though it seemed like minutes were passing. As the ringing in his head cleared, Rico patted himself down, searching for the impact, waiting for the pain that hadn't come yet. Had he missed? The ringing in his ears made everything feel underwater, distant, and unreal.

Rico was confused. He looked around for some clarity. He saw Mr. Bojangle. In typical Bojangle's style, he was the calm during the chaos. The one that never seemed to crack. Mr. Bojangle made eye contact and gave him a big smile. It was that old, mischievous smile that they had come to love. He saw the red blooming across the old man's shirt like a rose, growing out from a center thorn. In that frozen moment, Rico knew. The shot didn't miss Rico. Mr. Bojangle had chosen one final life to change. One last piece of hope to protect, to protect him.

Rico. It made no sense. At the same time, it was the only thing in the room that did.

A second shot shattered the moment, and Rico dove to the floor.

Dante's face registered surprise. He dropped the Desert Eagle, and his hand drifted up to where his chest was shattered. He pulled his fingers away and stared at the blood on them with curiosity as he fell. Lifeless before he hit the ground.

The already scared crowd scattered like startled birds, screams finally breaking through the gunshot's echo.

Rico looked up to see Tyrell, holding his own snub-nose .38 still smoking in the boy's trembling hands.

Rosa reached Tyrell first, gathering him close as the gun clattered to the floor. Rico moved to shield him from the sight of what he'd done, from what he'd had to become.

Maria and Luis were huddled together deep under the table, where Big Mac formed a living shield between them and the violence. Rico could see sobs rocking the mountain of a man who had made the impossible choice of protecting the children over his dearest friend.

Sofia fell to her knees beside Mr. Bojangle, her hands pressing desperately against the wound.

"Por favor," Sofia whispered, her desperate plea drowning in tears. "Please don't go. We have more dances."

Mr. Bojangle smiled that same gentle smile that had changed

all their lives. "Don't be sad for me, Sofia. I get to see my Sarah, and my Emily, and my Jacob." His blue eyes sparkled. "It's going to be OK," he winced in pain after his sentence.

"He needs you, Mac." Sofia reached back and tugged at Big Mac's shirt. "The children are safe now. Bo needs you."

Bo gripped Mac's hand. "And Marcus... I'm so proud of you and CJ. I love you boys. You are my sons, too. In all the crazy, God gave me you. I am so thankful. You know that, don't you? You know what you need to do now."

"I'll make sure it happens, Mr. Bojangle," Big Mac assured him. Tears poured from his eyes as his words came out quietly. "Don't carry any of that worry with you, now. You just -" A sob strangled the rest of his words.

"I'm just going to dance with my lady," Bo said with a smile. "I won't be far away. You'll see."

Across the room, Tyrell had collapsed into Rico's arms, as the weight of pulling that trigger owned him. "What have I done? What am I now?"

"No," Rico held him tight. He spoke firmly, willing the truth to take hold before the lie could take over Ty's world. "You are Tyrell Carter. You are my friend. You are not what happened here. Do you hear me, Ty? The cycle ends now. I promise you that."

Mr. Bojangle's voice came softly, like a prayer: "I have a lot of hope to leave behind. Won't need it where I'm going. Heaven's built from the stuff." He laughed a little, as it turned into a small cough. "I love you, Mac." With his massive hands, Mac lifted him so he could catch his breath. Bojangle looked up, almost as if he was looking through Mac. "It's so beautiful… You got this, my son, always remember, I believe… in you."

Then, the blue eyes that had taught them to dream again went dim. The lips that had told so many to hope, dream, and believe were now settled into a curved smile. As his breathing stopped and his chest, in the crimson-stained shirt, became still, you could hear the sobs of those, now suddenly aware of how much darker the world had become. But for Bo, the dream of being in the arms of his family once again was no longer a dream. Bojangle was home.

CHAPTER 27

A New Dance Partner

The phone call came three days after Big Mac boarded the plane carrying Mr. Bojangle home so he could be laid to rest beside Sarah and the kids.

"Mr. Rico Morales? This is Calvin Johnson from the Bojangle's Foundation." The voice was crisp and professional. "We have a lot to talk about."

"The Bojangle's Foundation?" Rico asked, rolling his shoulders to loosen up some of the stiffness. He had been on the phone a lot lately. Almost as much as he had sat across the table from uniformed strangers in a wholehearted attempt to put things right. The electronic bracelet on his ankle was part of the first steps to that goal. He couldn't say it was comfortable, but he knew it was far better than he deserved. "Who is this again?"

"This is Calvin Johnson, CJ to my friends. We haven't met yet, but I'll be flying out later this week to speak to you in person," the man said. He sounded nearly as exhausted as Rico felt. I know this is short notice, but I promise to give you all the details when I arrive. For now, you need to know that the funds are available for the rebuild. The contractors will arrive on Monday. Will it be a problem for you to meet onsite that morning? Mac should be there by late afternoon to help out. Evening at the latest."

"What are you talking about, what funds?" Rico gripped the phone tightly. Whatever this was, Rico had enough on his plate. Between working with local, state, and federal law enforcement to untangle the web Dante had woven over the city, doing his best to be a solid part of the support network that was trying to keep its feet under it now that Mr. Bojangle was gone, and just keeping his head above water, he wasn't sure he could fit any more in.

"The funds set aside for the center's repairs after the fire," CJ said. When the silence stretched out, he blew out a breath. "I take it we have more to talk about than I thought. Okay, I can work with that. The short version is that Mr. Bojangle had some very detailed and specific plans for the community that evolved as necessary. One contingency plan set up before his death involves you stepping into a more active role with the foundation. Another - let's call it a Plan B - was triggered when the fire broke out. That would be the rebuild funds. Since Big Mac is still overseeing other things, that makes you my point of contact."

"Man, I hate to break it to you, but I'm staring down some serious felony charges here. The only reason I'm in the open air right now is because I've been working with every badge ever created to pull down Dante's ring. Whatever Mr. Bojangle had in mind for me, I'm sure he didn't want to put a felon in charge of things around here," Rico barked out a laugh.

"We'll compare rap sheets when I get there," CJ said sarcastically. "Mr. Bojangle was a man who believed in second chances. He believed in big dreams. And, Rico, he believed in people. He saw something in you that makes you perfect for the job at hand, or I would be calling someone else right now. All you have to do is live up to the trust he put in you. That's what I try to do every day. Big Mac, too. You'll get used to it. All you have to do is be on site, meet the contractors, sign the contract so they can start work, meet a couple of supply trucks, and sign off on their loads so they can get paid. You will also be responsible for monitoring inventory management. Nothing that you haven't done before. You'll be working with legal supplies this time," CJ laughed at his own joke.

"And a bigger budget, too. And, unless you have some

issue with any of this, we will be onboarding you officially and sorting out your salary. I think you will find it comfortable."

Rico swallowed hard. "Salary, what are we talking?" Not sure he was ready for the answer.

"Mr. Jangles hand-picks his people. He understood that you might be giving up some of your dreams to join him on his. He was grateful for that sacrifice. Your pay will reflect that sacrifice. We can discuss the details when I arrive, but trust me, we are well compensated to help Mr. Jangles' dreams come true. If I were a gambling man, I'd bet you have a number in your head you think you are worth… trust me when I say, he, and we think you are worth more."

It was just silence on the phone for what seemed like minutes.

"Are you there?" asked CJ.
"Who are you people?" whispered Rico.

"It's a lot. Trust me, I know it's a lot," CJ replied softly. "I had hoped that Mr. Bojangle had time to explain it all to you already, but well… Plans have changed. Do you think you can handle jumping into the deep end of a crazy new adventure?"

"I'm going to have to," Rico nodded his head even though CJ couldn't see. "I owe Mr. Bojangle more than I can ever repay. If he needs this from me, I'll dive in headfirst and make it happen."

"Excellent," CJ said with more than a little relief. Big Mac will be there sometime tomorrow. He'll want everyone together at Rosa's. Can you add that to your to-do list?"

"Consider it done." Rico nodded again as his brain scrambled to balance everything.

When he hung up the phone, he blew out a breath that ended in a disbelieving laugh. Who knew that when the life you had known came crashing down around you, sometimes it was just so all the pieces could fall into the right place?

"I won't let you down, Mr. Bojangle," Rico whispered, knowing that somewhere, somehow, the man who had changed so many lives here was listening.

By the time Big Mac arrived at the burned-out husk of the center the next afternoon, Rico had everything well in hand.

"I'm sorry all of this landed in your lap before anyone could give you a heads up," Mac said with a yawn. "Losing Mr. Bojangle was a hard hit, and some things slipped through the cracks. Looks like you stepped up to the challenge just like he knew you would."

"I couldn't have done it if you and CJ hadn't convinced everyone to expand the range on this little beauty." Rico lifted his pant leg to show his ankle bracelet. "Funny how I used to dread the day I finally got caught. I don't think I've felt this free since I was a kid."

"I hear Spider was the first one they brought in," Mac said.

"Is it wrong that part of me wants this to be his wake-up call? That I want to pull him through and into better days once he's had time to think?" Rico asked.

"Nope." Mac's smile lit up his face like Christmas. "That is exactly the right idea. That's why you are now on our team."

And then, looking back at his leg, "CJ has already made some calls to sort that ankle bracelet problem for you. Soon come."

Mac, leading Rico by the arm, said, "Come on, let's go to Rosa's. I want to get this next part off my chest so I can get some hope of sleeping tonight."

CHAPTER 28

The Full Dance

When everyone arrived at the restaurant, it was the first time most had been here since he incident. Sofia and Rosa had spent the last couple of days trying to erase the memory of that day. As people walked in, they were met with hugs from their neighbors and genuine smiles from people happy to see them.

When Big Mac was ready, he stepped to the front, and all eyes turned to him as a hush moved through the restaurant. The intimidating hulk of a man was gone, replaced by someone who looked impossibly tired, weighted down by memories and responsibilities. Grief seeped out of him even though his eyes were dry.

"I know I have a lot of explaining to do. I am asking that you let me get through this without interruption if you can. It's not an easy story to tell, and I have been running through how to share this, the entire trip over here. I hope I do this right and that it is fair to him. You want to know who Mr. Bojangle was, who he really was?" His deep voice caught slightly. "Who he was before the worn-out shoes and ragged shirts? Before he danced through our lives with his strange magic?" Some in the crowd nodded.

Mac pulled out a binder with old newspaper clippings. He read out just a few of the headlines:

FROM HANDSHAKE TO EMPIRE: Childhood Buddies Daniel J. Meridian and Robert Jangle Transform Garage Venture into Industry Powerhouse.

Manufacturing Giants Scramble as Meridian-Jangle Partnership Secures Fifth Major Purchase This Quarter.

Meridian - Janbo Corp. Sells Manufacturing Portfolio in Landmark Billion-Dollar Investment Group Acquisition.

Jangle Corp Unveils Stock Trading App Set to Transform Financial Markets.

Tech Mogul "Bo" Jangle Makes Historic $50M Gift to Children's Hospital.

Billionaire Liquidates Business Empire in Wake of Family Tragedy.

"Robert 'Bo' Jangle… was my friend. He built an empire from nothing. He started in his garage with his best friend and became one of the largest manufacturing giants in the US. They sold out to some venture capitalists and went their separate ways. He dove back in to become a leader in the tech industry." Mac paused to put away the folder and pull out some notes he had scribbled. Public speaking was not his happy place, and this was not his happy topic. "Years later, he saw what the investors did to his company when he left. Shuttered, sold for pieces, his employees and their communities… all hope was crushed. Robert's choice of this community was no accident, and not his first project.

Marcus paused to let the chatter die down. "The papers called him a business genius. His employees called him 'Mr. Bo'Jangle.' His friends called him 'Bo.' His wife, Sarah… 'Honey.' His kids, Emily and Jacob…they called him 'Daddy.' He loved hearing Emily sing Disney songs at the top of her voice and made time to be in the backyard tossing a ball with his little Jacob as often as he could."

Mac's hands trembled slightly as he looked out at the faces - Rosa, Sofia, Rico, all the people whose lives had been touched by a crazy old man.

"His wife, Sarah, loved to dance. Bo would come home and dance with her in their kitchen after a crazy day. He said that was how they both found their center, and he was the happiest.

Each step of every dance led back to her, because she and the kids were his happiness."

The silence deepened. They all knew this story was going to lead to a place no one wanted to go, but they were underestimating it. Mac put his notes away. From here on out, he knew the story better than it was written.

"Then, there was a night that changed everything. The night when two desperate young men thought they were breaking into an empty house. The night when a man who had everything..." Mac's voice broke. He cleared his throat and started again. "The night when a man who had everything lost it all."

Rosa got up silently to get Big Mac a glass of water. He took a sip and took a deep breath. Sofia handed him a napkin so he could wipe away the tears that had gathered in his eyes.

"His home was incredible. They had just finished rehabbing a turn-of-the-century stone house with an old carriage garage. There were two intruders. The two thieves cut the power, thinking it would disable everything. It was supposed to be a simple job, in and out. Nobody was supposed to be home." Mac's voice grew softer as he reached the hardest part of the story. The room hung on every word. "Sarah... she was always trying to fix things herself. They heard her soft footsteps in the dark and saw the flicker of candlelight as she made her way across the dining room to the basement door to check the fuse box. She was humming that same tune when he danced." Rico noticed Big Mac's hands were shaking.

"The thieves tried to hide. They were so young and so damned stupid, and the plan they threw together was going to shit. All they wanted to do was get out of there. Just get out.

But the candlelight caught up with them first. They saw her face, and she saw theirs. Such kindness in her eyes, even in that moment of fear. Her scream... I still hear it. CJ and I panicked. The crowbar was just for opening windows, but..."

Everyone gasped. Sofia had her hand over her mouth. "The candle fell," Mac's voice hitched. He cleared his throat and forced himself to go on. "Oil-finished hardwood floors. Old furniture. It went up so fast. We ran. God help us, we ran."

The room fell into a profound silence, the air thick with the gravity of Big Mac's confession.

"Mr. Bojangle was at a late business meeting when his phone rang. A silent alarm had been tripped at his house. No one was answering. Emergency services were on their way. He didn't waste a second. All he knew was that he had to get home. The traffic was bad. When he reached his street, the flames were already through the roof. His neighbors had to hold him back. He kept screaming their names." Marcus wiped his eyes.

Rico went to sit beside Tyrell. The kid was barely hanging in there. The Jimmy, Bojangle, Dante... now Mac's story? Rico was mentally drained, but knew he needed to be there for Ty now. He just held him and rocked, as everyone cried tears together.

"When it was all done. They found them. Sarah had managed to get to the children's rooms. They found them together, Emily and Jacob, in their mother's arms. She'd tried to shield them from the smoke." Mac looked like he had shrunk into himself. As if telling everyone about that night was pulling him apart, deflating him with each word. "Robert died that night, too. The successful businessman, the loving father - it all burned away. I watched him fall in that yard from the back of a police cruiser. He spent three years in a haze of grief and bourbon. He disappeared into the alleys, talking to ghosts. CJ and I spent the same three years in lockup. We were the lucky ones." The silence in the room was absolutely cutting.

"Salvation," Marcus said softly. A smile, as full of peace as it was sadness, curved his lips. "Sometimes saving grace comes in the form of an old woman carrying a Tupperware soup container. A sweet lady named Katy found Mr. Bojangle sleeping in an alley behind her church. Instead of calling the police, she nursed him back to health. She wasn't afraid of his tangled beard and bourbon-soaked clothes. She saw the broken man beneath. Katy gave him a place to sleep, and she would make soup from her little vegetable garden for him.

The story came to an abrupt pause as the bell above the door sounded and everyone turned. In walked a middle-aged man, almost resembling Mac, but significantly shorter and not as strong. He had an almost clean-shaven head but just enough stubble for the grey that was starting on his temples to show through.

"I couldn't let you do this alone, Marcus," the man said. "I rearranged my schedule and got here as fast as I could. I hope you don't mind."

"Ah, CJ, it's so good to see you," Big Mac said, getting up to greet his friend with a bear hug. "And no, I don't mind at all. I wasn't sure I was going to get through it all on my own."

"Sit," CJ said, pulling up a second chair. "I'll take over the telling. Where did you leave off?"

"Katy had just rescued Bojangle, and I was moving to

Rikers." Mac closed his eyes and swallowed as if the memory of it was cutting off his air. "Should I introduce you first?"

"They already know who I am," CJ looked out at the people around him for confirmation. "They know my part up to this point. I'm the accountant, research director, legal wrangler, political advocate, and all-around 'whatever Bo needed done that wasn't on site' guy. I feel like I already know most of you. "

Rosa got up to get a second glass of water while CJ settled into the chair and took a deep breath. After thanking her, he nodded and repeated, "Rikers."

The crowd leaned forward, hanging on every word, trying to understand how their dancing stranger had come to love the men who destroyed his life.

"He came to Queens… to Rikers on a Tuesday," CJ said, his hands clasped to stop their shaking. "Mr. Robert 'Bo' Jangles, the man you knew as Mr. Bojangle, walked into that visiting room like a man going to an execution. Looking for monsters. Looking for reasons to keep hating."

CJ rubbed his right wrist nervously, a habit when the memories pressed too close. Everyone could tell he was trying to explain a past he desperately wished he didn't own.

"But he found something else instead. Two broken boys, drowning, holding the weight of their choices. He found Calvin Johnson, that would be me, sitting there in prison blues, still working math problems on napkins because his mind wouldn't stop solving equations even behind bars. I'm sorry for talking in the third person here. Crowds… are hard for me. Talking in front of people. I'm not doing it on purpose."

Rico and Ty made eye contact with CJ and just smiled, offering silent support as he struggled to continue.

"Calvin was supposed to be somebody. He had scholarships lined up and teachers fighting over who'd get to write his recommendations. Then one rainy night, a drunk driver didn't see the stop sign. Calvin's… my father died instantly, and grandma was left…" CJ shook his head. "You know, hospital bills piled up like crazy, and she had been let go from the factory when the new company bought it. How were we supposed to make it? The gang had been watching me for months, knowing I was good with numbers and could help their operation. They offered salvation. I could take care of the bills and Grandma, if I just gave a little of my soul."

A sob broke the silence. Ty was still trying to hold it together, but CJ's story wasn't far from his own truth. Jamal went to join Rico at his side with as much support as he could offer.

"Mr. Bojangle sat there for hours on that first visit, just listening. Not to hear excuses, but to try to understand, hear the story of how hope dies. How good intentions crack under pressure. How one decision can change a life. How one bad choice leads to another until you're so far from who you were meant to be, you can't find your way back."

Marcus stood, his massive frame casting shadows on the wall. CJ nodded. He knew Big Mac's road to this moment mattered, and that he was the only one who could tell it. "Brother, the floor is yours."

"I was always my mom's protector," Mac said softly. "Even as a boy. My father left when I was four. Mama would tell me to stand tall. She would tell me I was the man of the house now. I didn't understand, as a little boy, how hard it was to carry a man's burden. We didn't have much, but we had each other. My mom worked two jobs - a diner by day and cleaning offices at night. I would wait up, no matter how late, just to make sure she got home safe."

Everyone in the room knew that more bad was coming. It hung in the air the same way the acrid scent of charred wood hovered over the ruins of the Community Center.

"It was April 15th. Almost midnight. Mama was tired, so tired she wasn't paying attention. She didn't notice them following her from the bus stop. They waited until she unlocked the door and then pushed her inside. She closed her eyes when it started and tried not to scream. She didn't want them to know I was upstairs. Didn't want me to come down to see what was happening. She was doing her best to protect me, but it didn't work. I heard a muffled whimper and went downstairs, because that's what the man of the house was supposed to do. When I saw them, I just snapped and attacked, trying to protect my mom."

The silence stretched, heavy with unspoken pain.

"There were two of them. Big men." His fingers brushed over the scar on his face unconsciously. "It was really bad. They made sure they marked her up when they were done. Hurt her bad enough that all she could do was curl into herself and pray for it all to end." He paused, closed his eyes as another tear broke and ran down his cheek. "And then they hurt me too, real bad. I have this scar you can see… and some you can't."

He continued with a quiver in his voice as he made this confession. It was both painful and cathartic, making his story public, probably for the first time. Sobs came from all around the room as he continued the tale.

"The police came after enough of the neighbors called about

the screaming. They made reports. But in our neighborhood? We were just two more victims. Two more files in a drawer somewhere."

Everyone in the room understood. Everyone had a file in a drawer somewhere, but there wasn't enough manpower to give them the justice they needed. There might as well have been a black hole waiting to swallow the forms. The police were just as helpless as the victims to stop the crime.

"I used to be a good boy. I was kind, loving. I helped old ladies with their groceries. I was a gangly kid wearing his cousin's hand-me-down pajamas even past when they fit. I dreamed of being a teacher." Marcus slammed his palm down on the table and then paused to pull himself back together. "I was her protector, but I couldn't save her, and she was mine, and she couldn't save me. What they took from me that night." His voice went high as he tried not to cry. "She didn't even make it to the hospital that night. They hurt her so bad. They took too much from her. They took her from me. They took too much from me." Mac paused to gain his composure from the tears he failed to hold back. He knew he was past the hardest part. His voice grew stronger as he continued.

"All I had was hate. I wanted my power back, but with no hope after Mama was gone, I didn't see how. The gang promised me protection. Said my size and my face earned me that. They saw my anger and knew how to use it. They said power would come if I followed the rules and did what I was told. I was now a soldier." Mac walked over to the window and stared out.

"Mr. Bojangle stood, and with the gentle grace, took us both in his arms and let us cry for the first time." CJ rubbed his wrist thoughtfully. "He told us we were the two bravest boys he had ever known. He said it was time, past time, for us to heal. He came looking for demons to hate. Instead, he found two little boys, one trying to save Grandma, and one protecting his mama from the monsters. He found us. And in finding us, he found himself again."

The silence in Rosa's restaurant was broken only by quiet tears and sobbing. Their old hero had been more than just a man with a mission; he had been redemption wearing worn-out shoes, hope disguised as a vagrant, love masquerading as a dancing Santa Claus, quietly seeking his own redemption too.

"That's why he came here," CJ said softly. "Not just to help, not just to try to make good, but to show everyone that second chances aren't just possible - they're necessary. That forgiveness isn't just about letting go of hate but building something new from the ashes of what was lost."

He looked around the room at all the lives Mr. Bojangle had touched, all the dreams he'd rekindled. Big Mac came back to the table and retook his seat.

"He gave CJ and me more than freedom. He gave us purpose. He became like our dad, too. He loved us. And that showed us how to love. And now, he's gone. He's gone because that kind of love matters. It's all that matters." Big Mac took the hand that Sofia reached out to him gently. "Now it's time that we teach that secret to everyone else. That's our job."

"He made us promise to carry on his work. To believe in others the way he believed in us." CJ's tears fell freely now. "And that's exactly what we're going to do."

"Tell us where to start," Rosa said.

With her words, the room erupted in questions, all of them about what they could do to carry on Mr. Bojangle's mission.

Big Mac and CJ looked at each other for a long moment, smiles breaking through their tears. This was exactly what Mr. Bojangle would have wanted to see happen. This was the second chance everyone needed.

CHAPTER 29

A New Dance Begins

Some say you measure a person's life by what they leave behind. One year after Mr. Bojangle's final bow, his footprints had become foundations, his dreams had become reality, and his belief in second chances had rewritten the story of an entire neighborhood, sending ripples of light into the city it belonged to.

The morning sun caught the fresh paint on Jamal's mural, a three-month project stretching two stories high on the rebuilt brick of Mr. Bojangle's old home. He'd insisted on mixing the blue for the eyes himself, spending weeks getting it just right - that particular shade of hope that had looked into so many broken lives and seen only possibility. He saw the potential in Jamal. His new company had been hired to do murals on a few key buildings around town, and even a couple of big rollers upstate that CJ knew, reached out to engage his services.

The Jimmy Riley Sports Complex echoed with the crack of bats and children's laughter. Coach Rico stood at home plate, adjusting a young pitcher's grip and preparing for the final pitch. The boy's form was perfect, just like Tyrell had taught him before he headed off to college on his baseball scholarship.

Rico took a moment as the ball sailed through the air to think of Spider. He went every week during visiting hours. He would continue to do so until the cracks he was starting to see in Spider's hard shell opened enough to start letting the light in. Once that happened, Rico would make sure that the spark continued to grow. Continued to heal. After all, it would have been easy enough for their roles to be reversed, and Rico understood the shadows. He knew how to drive them back. Maybe the man Spider should have been, had a chance to come alive.

Through open windows, Sofia's piano merged with María's

voice. They were teaching a new generation of neighborhood kids that music is magical. The music school, once just wishful thinking, now filled most of the first floor, greeting all who came with the sound of joy. Sometimes, during lessons, Sofia would catch herself plucking out that old tune, the one she and Mr. Bojangle had danced to. The tune that helped her remember who she was and who she had become again.

Rosa's new café was just next door. Somehow, even with the new location, it still felt like home. It buzzed with life as it looked over the ballpark. Luis darted between tables, simultaneously waiter, cashier, and dishwasher, pausing only to check the clock for baseball practice time. Rosa watched him with proud eyes, remembering someone else who'd once fixed toys and believed in possibilities.

"Full house today," Rico observed, joining Marcus at their usual table in the new café. "I'll take a big iced tea, please. It's a hot one out there."

"Angel will be in to help out just as soon as he gets cleaned up," Rosa said sweetly. "Maria had him on dog-walking duty this morning, and he was covered in slobber. And Avril will be in after school to take over, so I can attend today's dance lesson. The teacher can't be late, can she? That sweet girl is even bringing a couple of friends to interview. It's a good thing Luis's got so much energy. He's been amazing while I'm trying to get fully staffed, but I'll be glad to see the day when he can do kid things instead. I hear a soapbox derby is coming up at the end of summer that he plans to win."

"So, Rosa and Angel?" Rico smiled as Rosa spun away with a wink to get the next order out.

"Mr. Bojangle was never wrong," Big Mac grinned. He looked out the big windows at all he had helped create and let the smile grow. "I love watching the neighborhood bloom."

Rico nodded. He watched as David and Ethan gave a tour of the sports center to a new family. "Jimmy would've loved this. All of it."

"He sees it," Mac said softly. "They all do."

The afternoon light painted everything gold. It was a reminder that some things would always be precious and pure. Through the window, they could see Tyrell's younger brother throwing pitches, wearing his big brother's old glove. The ugly cycle of shadows breaking, one dream at a time.

"Do you think he knew?" Rico asked suddenly. The question had been weighing on him for far too long. He needed to get it off his chest. "Mr. Bojangle. About Dante? About what would happen?"

Marcus was quiet for a long moment, his scarred face thoughtful. "I think he knew what mattered. That one day, he would be with Sarah and the kids. I think he knew that when he left, he had people ready to carry on his dream. People who understood what it means to believe."

"That's you, me, and CJ now." Rico stood, straightening his coaching jacket. "We got a lot of work to do."

"There will be others when the time is right to bring them in. For now, we do have a lot to do. The plane is coming to pick us up tomorrow, early, so get a good night's rest, Rico. I haven't managed to pack yet, so I'd better get on that soon." Big Mac unfolded himself from the booth, which was now his special table for when he came in. "CJ needs the next phase hashed out quickly, so expect a long day of planning. And he has pulled the research for that community outside of Springfield. We're gonna be busy!" he said with a smile and popped Rico on the shoulder.

They walked out together, past the ballpark where Jimmy's name stood proud on the sign, past Sofia's music school, where dreams had learned to sing again. They passed where the new veterinarian office was breaking ground near the sign hanging over Katy's Community Garden.

They stopped at the mural, looking up at those eyes that somehow Jamal got to twinkle even in paint. The setting sun caught the silver in the big silver beard, making it shine like a beacon. Below, in an elegant script that seemed to glow in the twilight, were the words that had changed everything:

"I believe in you."

A grand reminder to believe in second chances. They looked up at the sunset. "The sky looks different when you have someone you miss up there." Said Big Mac, and Rico agreed.

"I miss him too, but you know what he is doing."

"I do, I do know what he's doing."

And somewhere, in the space between memory and hope, between what was lost and what was found, an old man danced, in the crack of every bat, in the sound of every piano key, in the laughter of children who might never know his name but would live out his legacy.

With a heart full of hope and forgiveness, wearing worn-out shoes, Mr. Bojangle was dancing.

ABOUT THE AUTHOR

M.C. Keesee is an Oklahoma boy who traded prairie sunsets for Caribbean breezes but never lost his down-to-earth soul. A storyteller by trade and dreamer by nature, he writes about hope that's been tested and redemption that's been earned, because he has walked both of those roads. His stories speak of second chances (because he needed them) and grit (because he knows grace isn't cheap). But his proudest titles? Devoted husband. Proud father. Loyal friend. Humbled man of faith.

To M.C., Life's real treasures are simple but sacred: a great dinner shared with kindred spirits, late-night patio conversations with his beautiful wife, and bedtime prayers with his sons.

These days, you'll find him somewhere between palm trees and prairie memories, still chasing dreams, scribbling down ideas, and counting blessings. (Far more than he deserves.)

ACKNOWLEDGEMENTS

My first thanks go to God. He continues to author my story, and I am thankful for the blessings he keeps writing for this protagonist. Thank you to my incredible wife, Anita. You are my cheerleader, my critic, my muse and my best friend. Your patience with my late-night writing sessions made this possible. David and Ethan, you inspire me daily, Daddy loves you!

To my early readers, Jeremy, Nylah, Ivy, and Cathy, who saw Bojangle's potential, thank you for your faith in this story.

To the team who helped shape Bojangle's journey, Brittney and Kristal...my most profound appreciation.

Bojangle lives because of you.

And to you, holding this book...thank you for letting Bojangle's Dance into your world.